SCORNED BY THE LOVE
OF A THUG

BY:

NATIONAL BESTSELLING AUTHOR,

MZ. BIGGS

SCORNED BY THE LOVE OF A THUG

Check Out These Other Great Books By Mz. Biggs:

See What Had Happened Was: A Contemporary Love Story (Part: 1-3)

Yearning For The Taste of A Bad Boy (Part: 1-3)

Dirty South: A Dope Boy Love Story (Part: 1)

Falling for A Dope Boy (Part: 1-3)

Feenin' For That Thug Lovin' (Part: 1-3)

A Bossed Up Valentine's (Anthology)

Jaxson and Giah: An Undeniable Love (Part: 1-2)

Finding My Rib: A Complicated Love Story (Part: 1)

In love With My Cuddy Buddy (Part: 1-2/Collaboration)

Your Husband's Cheating On Us (Part: 1-3)

From Cuddy Buddy To Wifey: Levi and Raven's Story (Standalone/Collaboration)

In Love With My Father's Boyfriend (Standalone)

Your Husband's Calling Me Wifey (Standalone)

She's Not Just A Snack... She's A Whole Buffet: BBWs Do It Better (Standalone)

Blood Over Loyalty: A Brother's Betrayal (Standalone)

Scorned By The Love Of A Thug

Married to the Community D (Part: 1-2)

Downgraded: From Wifey to Mistress (Part: 1-3)

A Mother's Prayer (Part: 1-2)

Heart of A Champion... Mind Of A Killer (Standalone)

Turned Out By My Husband's Best Man (Standalone)

Ain't No Lovin' Like Gulf Coast Lovin' On The 4th of July (A Novella)

This Is Why I Love You (A Novella)

The Hood Was My Claim To Fame (A Novella)

A Killer Valentine's (Anthology)

Bouncing Back After Zaddy Gave Me The Clap (Standalone)

Tantalizing Temptations in New Orleans (An Erotic Novella)

Santa Blessed Me With a Jacktown Boss (Novella)

Diamonds and Pearls (Standalone)

Dating A Female Goon (Standalone/Collaboration)

Pregnant By My Best Friend's Husband (Part: 1-2)

Wifed Up By A Down South Boss (Thug Love Collection/Anthology)

Creepin' With The Plug Next Door (Part: 1-3)

Creepin' With My Co-Worker (Part 1)

Scorned By The Love Of A Thug

Crushin' On A Dope Boy: Cashae and Tay (Anthology)

The Autobiography of A Boss's Wife (Collaboration)

Author's Note:

Please take the time to leave an honest review on either Amazon or Goodreads after reading the book. Your support is greatly appreciated. Also, feel free to reach out to me anytime via the contact information listed below. Happy Reading... ☺

~Mz. Biggs

Want to connect with me? Here's how:

Email: authoress.mz.biggs@gmail.com

Twitter: @mz_biggz

Instagram: mz.biggs

Goodreads: Mz. Biggs

Facebook: https://www.facebook.com/authoress.biggs

Author Page: https://www.facebook.com/MzBiggs3/

Look for my Reading Group on Facebook: Lounging with Mz. Biggs

Chapter One:

Mignon

"Damn ma, you look good as hell," my boyfriend, Javi told me. "Stand up and let me see what you're working with," he instructed as he licked his lip. This man was sexy as hell to me. Every time we were able to see each other, it seemed like his ass had gotten finer and finer.

Javi was five feet, eight inches tall. Normally, men over six feet were my desired preference. However, there was just something about Javi that I could never shake. It was his swag. Dope boy mentality. Thug passion. Shit, I didn't know. Whatever it was, I was here for it.

Javi had a smile that could light up a whole room when he entered. He was very muscular, with washboard abs, and a mocha skin complexion. His whole bottom row of teeth was decked out in gold, but he only had four gold teeth on the top. They were on his incisors; the four teeth in the front. In the past, I would've walked right past him. There were too many pictures floating around about how people with gold teeth had rotten teeth and gums underneath and I didn't want to risk growing old with someone whose gums were too rotten to even get dentures. The thought of it made me laugh.

"What's so funny?" Javi asked.

"Nothing, I was just thinking about something," I replied.

"Thinking about what?" he continued to probe. He had a mean expression on his face. If you knew anything about Javi, you'd know that he was very impatient and wanted everything his way.

We'd been together for the last five years, but he'd been in jail for two and a half of those years. Prison actually. I'd made it to every visitation, kept money on his books, and accepted every phone call. You can't imagine how many miles I've put on my car and how much my phone bill has been. Besides that, I've also managed to save all the money I've gotten from school refunds, income taxes, and any money that I had left after paying my bills, just so I could afford a good attorney for him. It was no secret that having an attorney assigned to you, better known as a public defender, was like signing a death warrant.

"Baby, you hear me?" Javi asked, removing me from my thoughts.

"Yeah. I'm anxious. I can't wait for you to go to court. There's no reason they wouldn't let you out, is there?" I replied, changing the subject.

"Hell no. They got me on some trumped-up ass charges. You know like I know that I've never raped anybody. This some bullshit and you know it."

You heard correctly. Javi was out with some friends one night and they met some women at a club. I don't know what happened after that because Javi asked me to stay out of the courtroom whenever witnesses testified as to what transpired after they left the club. The one thing I did know was that the women claimed that they were raped that night. Javi told me they were lying and since I'd never had a reason to doubt anything he said to me, I believed him.

"Besides, why would I need to steal pussy when I've got yours? That shit is as addictive as oxycodone," he expressed, causing me to smile.

"Thank you. I can't wait until you're out of here. I need you home with me. Plus, I'm tired of working all of these long ass hours. I work two jobs just to stay afloat with paying my bills and your attorney fees."

"Your reward is in heaven, baby. God will give everything back to you two-fold."

There was no way I heard his ass correctly. His ass had never been to church, never prayed, and was a fuckin' atheist, but had the nerve to bring God up. Where they do that at?

"You can stop trying to patronize me. You really don't care about what I'm doing for you as long as it gets done, right?"

"You know it's not like that. It's jus-"

"It's just what?" I interrupted him.

"It's just that I can't do anything for you in here. You know if I was out, I'd be bringing home all the money so you can focus solely on school. I'm going to make this shit up to you. It's only right because you've held me down and remained faithful the whole time I've been in here. I couldn't have asked for a better woman to be by my side through all of this," he stated.

It would've been great if I were listening to everything that he was saying, but I couldn't. For some reason, there was some strange ass woman sitting at the table behind us, staring me up and down.

"Why does she always do that?" I finally had the courage to ask Javi after trying my best to ignore it during previous visits.

"Why do who always do what?"

"Why does this chick behind us keep staring me up and down?" I probed.

"Maybe she wants you," he chuckled.

"Nigga don't play with me. I don't eat tuna."

"If you can eat it out of the can, you can eat it out of her panties." I looked at him sideways before punching him in the shoulder.

"Keep your hands to yourself," one of the guards yelled.

"My bad," I exclaimed. He acted like I was slobbering Javi down or something. That was another reason I was going to be glad when he got out of here. I'd be able to touch him whenever I wanted and however, I wanted.

"Don't be apologizing to him, we ain't do nothing wrong," Javi fired back. The guard stepped closer to us like he wanted to say something. Javi stood from his seat. I had no choice but to stand as well. He didn't need any more problems while he was going through this trial. If his ass got in trouble again and had to serve more time for new charges, he was on his own. Shit, I loved him and was willing to be his ride or die, but not when his ass was in the wrong.

"Sit down, Javi. We only have a few more minutes left for visitation and I don't want any issues."

"Yeah, aight. You better be glad my girl saved your ass," he said to the guard. He got on my damn nerves with always thinking he had to have the last word in. The shit was sad. One day he was going to open his mouth to talk and someone was going to knock his fuckin' tongue down his throat.

"Sit your ass down," I told him and snatched his ass down to his seat. He kept his eye on the guard and I kept my eyes on the unknown female.

"Can I have my face back?" I finally asked, after growing tired of her staring at me.

"Sorry, you look familiar to me," she told me.

"Then you could've just said something. You didn't have to stare at me like that," I replied.

"You're right. I'm sorry," she repeated. I gave her a half smile and turned my attention back on Javi who was still staring at the guard.

"I'm going to go on back to my cell before this nigga make me fuck him up," Javi finally spoke. Normally, I would've argued with him, but not this time. Something felt off to me.

We both stood from our seats. He pulled me in for a hug and a kiss even though he knew we weren't supposed to be touching. The guard yelled out to us again and I pulled away from Javi. Walking towards the door, I turned back to blow him another kiss before I exited. As I was walking down the long hallway to be checked out before I left, it dawned on me that I'd left my jacket.

"I'm sorry, I left my jacket," I told the guard that was walking behind me. He turned me around and walked back to the visitation room with me. When the door opened for me to step inside, I froze in my tracks. The same woman that had been staring with me was sitting and laughing with Javi. Like a lion quietly searching for its next meal, I crept up on them. "What's going on here?" I asked once I was in their presence.

"Baby, this is Shawnte. Shawnte, this is my friend, Mignon," he called himself introducing us.

"Friend?" That caught me off guard. We hadn't been friends in five years and all the money I've forked out to help his ass proved that we were more than friends.

"She's knows what you are to me, baby."

"That's cool, but why is she over here?"

"She came over to apologize again for the way she was looking at you. Then we got to talking about you and how much you've done for me." My eyes darted over to her. She was frowned up when I peeked at her but when she noticed I was looking, she quickly turned her frown into a smile. I acted as if I didn't see it, but please believe me when I say that game recognized game. She was on some shady shit and so was Javi. If I found out that his wanna be thug as was on some bullshit, he was going to pay dearly for the shit.

"Whatever. I'll stand here until you go back to your cell or until she leaves."

"Are you saying you don't trust me?"

"No, I'm saying I don't trust her and right now, you're giving me a million and one reasons not to trust you. If I were you, I'd tiptoe my black ass back to my damn cell and find something safe to do." I kissed him on the cheek and waited for him to respond. After a few moments, he turned on his heels and walked towards the door leading to the back of the prison. It wasn't until he was out of my sight and the woman had left that I finally exited the visitation room.

Now, I don't know about other women, but I knew for sure that my ass wasn't on no dumb shit. Javi had me fucked up if he thought I was going to let his ass be snickering and grinning with the next bitch. Now, if she would've contributed to helping with his attorney's fees and making sure he was good, then I probably wouldn't have said shit, but since that wasn't the case, she needed to bounce her bubble body ass back to where she came from. I may be a lot of things but a fuckin' fool wasn't one.

Chapter Two:

Mignon

(Two Weeks Later)

The day had finally arrived for Javi to go to court. I'd still managed to make it to every visitation, answered every phone call, put money on his books, pay off his attorney's fees, and be the woman I'd always vowed to be.

Last night was draining for me. I was so anxious to get to court because I had high hopes my baby would end up being released today. So, of course, I stayed up all damn night. I made sure the house was cleaned from top to bottom. I made sure that the clothes I'd purchased for him throughout the years were neatly placed in the closet so he could have his own space.

Javi was doing pretty good for himself when he was working the streets. The minute he was arrested, he lost everything. Even the money he left with his mother vanished. That wasn't surprising considering she'd pulled a disappearing act herself. You read that correctly. Javi's mother took his money and hauled ass.

Javi was the only child. He'd assumed that he and his mother had a pretty decent relationship. That was until he was locked up and not once did she pay towards his attorney's fees, visit him, answer a call, appear in court to speak on his behalf, or put money on his damn books. About a week after he was locked up, I paid her a visit to make sure she was good and to see if there was anything I could do for her. Imagine my surprise when I got to her home and all of her shit was gone. Apparently, nobody knew where she'd gone or if her ass was coming back. She'd gotten her phone cut off so there was no way of tracking her or even reaching out to her. Shit, that wasn't my place to do anyways. I'm sure if Javi wanted to know where she was bad enough, he had more than enough connections to find her.

Dragging myself out of bed, I walked towards the windows and let my blinds up. The sun shined brightly in my face. It was so bright, I had to close my eyes and turn away from the window to clear my vision. That sun could blind the fuck out of you.

Ring... Ring... Ring...

The sound of my phone ringing reminded me that I was supposed to call my mother last night. She was the only person that could call me this early in the morning and I wouldn't get upset. That was because the bond we had was solid as hell.

"Good Morning Mom. I'm sorry about last night. I know I was supposed to call you, but I had too much on my mind," I rattled off into the phone.

"Bitch, I'm not old enough to be your mother," my best friend Robin screeched.

"My bad. I answered without checking to see who it was. What you doing up so early?" I asked. Robin and I had been best friends for as long as I could remember. She was a true rider for real. Her being up so early was shocking to me because she always stayed up until 3 or 4 in the morning and never woke up until it was close to 1 in the afternoon. How she did it, I'd never know. I knew my ass couldn't do it, so I never bothered to try.

"Girl, it's a big day for you. Did you really think I was going to allow you to walk in the courtroom alone?"

"I honestly thought that you forgot," I told her.

"How the hell could I forget when you've reminded me every day for the past two damn weeks. Not to mention the fact that you practically threatened to beat my ass if I weren't there for you," she replied. I couldn't help but laugh.

"Why you bringing up old shit?" I questioned her, still giggling.

"That shit ain't old. You just did it last night, hoe," she retorted. While I was laughing, I noticed that she was not, so I stopped. At least I stopped laughing loud enough for her to hear.

"What time are you supposed to be there?"

"Court starts at 9. I'm going around 8:15 so I can find a good parking spot and get inside the courtroom before all of the good seats are taken."

"Okay. Well you need to leave a little earlier so you can come scoop me up."

"Scoop you up? Unh uh. If my man's shit is thrown out, then I'm going to wait for him to be released so we can fuck all in the parking lot. I haven't had sex in two and a half years, we have a lot of making up to do," I confessed.

"I could've gone the rest of my life without hearing that," she told me.

"Whatever hoe. You do more fuckin' than me," I spat.

"That's because I'm not tied down to one nigga and even if I was, his ass better not leave room for another nigga to step in and take his place. Holding that nigga down for two and a half years is crazy as fuck to me. What if he doesn't stay with you when he gets out?" That was the first time she'd ever said anything to me like that. I'd never thought about the fact that Javi could turn on me. After all the shit that I'd gone through for him, if his ass did turn on me, I'd have to fuck him up. That's, 'On God'.

Glancing over at the time, it read 6:37. I was irritated about having to get up so early, but that gave me enough time to get myself together, put something on my stomach, and pick Robin's crazy ass up.

"Be ready at 7:45 or your ass is left," I told her and hung up the phone without allowing her the chance to say something smart.

The moment I put my phone down, I rushed to get done what I needed to get done. There really wasn't much time for me to really eat since it took me forever to do my makeup, so I just ate some toast and jelly. That was so I could at least say that I put something on my stomach.

Making sure I had everything I needed, I ran out the house being sure to lock up behind me. I threw my purse on the backseat and got in the car. Starting it up, I threw it in reverse to ba ck out of my driveway and into Robin's driveway. She lived right next door.

Beep... Beep... Beeeeppppppppp...

I laid on the horn because it was 8:30 and we still had to get to the court to find somewhere to park and a seat inside the courtroom, all before 9:00. Glancing up, I noticed Robin running out of her house with her shoes in her hand and her wig twisted. I shook my head at her before laughing.

"What's funny hoe?" she asked when she jumped inside the car.

"That damn wig that's about to fly off your fuckin' head," I replied, pointing at her head.

"Girl, Darius was trying to get in a damn quickie this morning and made me late," she explained.

"Darius? Who the hell is that?" I queried.

"It's a long story that we shall talk about at a later date and time," she smirked.

"Whatever. Put your seatbelt on so we can go." It wasn't long before we were on our way. Thankfully, traffic wasn't too bad, so it didn't take us long to get there. Especially, not after the way I was driving.

When Robin and I made it to the courthouse, an eerie feeling fell upon me. It was as if something were about to happen that I was unaware of.

"I'm going to go meet with his attorney, you go find us a seat," I told Robin. She shook her head and headed towards the courtroom as I sat on the benches in the hallway. I knew his attorney would have to walk past me, so I patiently waited to see him. I wanted to speak with him to see what I should expect from court on today.

The longer I sat on the bench and anticipated what the outcome of the day would be, the more my nerves started to get the best of me. Javi wasn't a bad guy at all. He just got caught up hanging with the wrong crowd which most people often did.

One night he linked up with one of his old friends and some other guys that he'd never met before and it caused his whole life to change. Even the people who we thought really knew him questioned his innocence, which he claimed since day one. He'd been asked what happened that night a thousand times and not once did anything in his story change. Still, people turned their backs on him.

Yeah, some of the events of the night seemed a bit farfetched, rather some things didn't add up, but we weren't there. Nobody could tell us what really happened but Javi, his friends, and the women. None of it mattered to me. My baby and I had been thick as thieves since day one and that wasn't going to change. If he said he was innocent, then I was rolling with it. Even if I would've seen him commit the crime and he still said he was innocent, then gotdamn it, his ass was innocent.

The clanking of some shoes walking towards me almost caused me to look up, but I didn't because I already knew who it was. His attorney, Mr. Latimore, always wore these shoes that made it sound like he was tap dancing when he walked. I kept my head down because there was something about Mr. Latimore that I didn't like. If I didn't make eye contact with him, then maybe he'd miss seeing me and keep walking right on pass. Yeah, I wanted to meet with him, but I kept having this bad feeling that I just couldn't shake.

"Ms. Tatum?" *Damn*, I thought to myself. Not once did I lift my head. Instead, I started fidgeting with my hands to make it appear as though I didn't hear him. "Ms. Tatum?" he said again. This time, he tapped me on the shoulder.

"Huh?" My head popped up. "Oh, hey Mr. Latimore," I said with a fake smile on my face.

"How are you feeling today?" he asked.

"Nervous," I replied. "How does everything look?" I added, taking a glimpse of the tight pinstriped suit he was wearing. It reminded me of one of those Steve Harvey suits, except his was super tight. It was a wonder his ass could breath.

"Hold on," he told me and walked over to where the security guards were standing. "Are you ready?" he came back over to me and asked.

"No, I'm not. Everyone is pretty much saying he's guilty and those people on the jury seem to be thinking the same thing. How can we get him out of this?" I quizzed.

"I'm going to be real honest with you, Mignon." He started talking and then abruptly stopped. "I'll be right back," he told me and walked away again. My eyes followed his every move, up until the time he came back and asked me to follow him

Mr. Latimore lead me inside of a room that looked like a small library. It was actually a mini law library with all these law and reference books and shit.

"Ms. Tatum, I'm going to be real honest with you. Your boyfriend is claiming to be innocent, but all of the evidence is stacked against him."

"What the hell is that supposed to mean? If he says that he's innocent and you don't even believe him, then I know he's screwed. You're his attorney. You should never say anything other than he's innocent," I yelled, pounding my hand on the table.

"I'm a public defender. You nor your boyfriend is paying me for this case. You get what you pay for," Mr. Latimore had the nerve to say to me.

My words suddenly became caught in my throat. What the hell did he mean by nobody was paying him? All of those extra shifts I took on, selling my shit, and saving all the money that I did to pay his fees and now he wants to tell me that he wasn't being paid. Surely, he knew he had me fucked up.

"What the hell do you mean by that? I know I've sent money to pay your ass several times so what is with this public defender shit?" I questioned. I was furious on the inside at the way he was coming at me and for lying about not getting any money out of me. His bucktoothed ass had better guess again if he thought he was about to skip town with my money.

"I'm not sure who you thought you were paying but I can assure you that it wasn't me. You may need to speak with your lying ass boyfriend," he spat.

Now, there was a part of me that could get real ratchet and real hood, real quick. I found myself looking around the room to see if there was anyone else in there that his ass could've been getting smart with. When I didn't see anyone, I knew for sure that he had fucked up by talking to me like he was crazy.

"Who you talking to Mr. Latimore?" I asked him after several minutes. "Regardless to whether we paid you or not, somebody is paying your ass and you still have a job to do. It's supposed to be done at the best of your ability. It seems to me that your ass already had him pegged as guilty from the jump and you're ready for this case to be over. I guess that's why you were pushing him so much to take that plea. Well guess what Mr. Latimore." I leaned across the table and grabbed ahold of his tie. I stared into his eyes because I wanted to make sure he was attentive to what I was about to say to him.

"Yes, Ms. Tatum."

"Fuck you and your plea. You're just mad because you can't find any other place to employ your overweight ass. Be thankful for the little tax money you done got from each and every person in our community, including my boyfriend's and mine."

Turning on my heels, I quickly exited the room. He called out behind me, but I was too pissed to respond. I didn't know if I needed to be madder at Javi for leading me to believe that he was using my money to pay for an attorney or at Mr. Latimore for not telling me that he was a damn public defender.

As I was heading back towards the courtroom, Javi was being brought in by four guards. The shackles that he wore on his wrists and ankles made me cringe. That was no way for a human to have to walk. They were treating him like an animal, and I didn't like that at all.

"He's not going to do anything. Do you have to make him wear those?" I asked, pointing at the shackles. "I promise he won't run," I tried reasoning with them.

"We are just doing our jobs, ma'am. Please step aside," one of the guards said to me. He reached out like he was about to touch me. Immediately, I pulled my phone out and went live on Facebook. If he was going to do something to me for no reason, then I was going to make sure other people saw it.

"All I did was ask a question. Don't put your damn hands on me," I spat. He looked at me and pulled his hand back like he was going to smack me. "I wish the fuck you would," I warned him.

"You need to move. Jace, come handle this. How did she even get in here with a cell phone? They are forbidden inside this building." Javi never said anything to support me. He shook his head and acted like he didn't know me.

"I'm not doing anything wrong. Why can't I have my phone?"

"This is a federal building and cell phones are not allowed. There is a sign that says that right as you walk in.

Either you can take it back to the car or they can confiscate it. The choice is yours."

"Fine. I'll take it back to my car. Don't worry, you have not seen the last of me."

"I'm sure we wouldn't dare be that lucky," he commented.

The guards pushed past me as I was on my way back to my car. It bothered me that not once did Javi say anything to defend me or try to get me to calm down. That was out of character for him. I wanted to say something, but I figured that it had something to do with his nerves. Maybe he was worried about the trial and didn't know what to say to me. I was being selfish thinking about my feelings and not his. That was something I was going to have to apologize to him about later.

Standing there, my eyes never left Javi as he was being led inside the courtroom. Instead of going back to my car, I surveyed the room to see if anyone was watching me before I turned my phone off and tucked it inside my bra. Then I took a deep breath and walked inside the courtroom behind them. The room was packed, but luckily, I was smart enough to have Robin find us a seat. I went right over to her and sat down beside her.

"it's going to be okay, sis. Your man is coming home today," she tried to assure me. Hearing that sounded good, but I still couldn't shake the feeling that something was about to go wrong.

Silently, I closed my eyes and prayed. That was all I could do.

Chapter Three:

Javi

The guards woke me up early as hell to get to the courthouse. It was a morning I'd been waiting for but also one that I wasn't ready for. The women claimed they were raped that night but them hoes gave us the pussy willingly. Like I told Mignon, why the fuck would I have to rape someone when I had her pussy at home, and I could get it anytime I wanted?

When I stepped inside the courthouse, I dropped my head because I didn't feel like looking at all those flashing cameras. The shit was a major case because the women just so happened to be white. Yeah, my homeboys and I fucked up that night. I tell you what though. You won't ever have to worry about my ass looking at white meat anymore, not even on a fuckin' chicken.

"Step this way, Javi," my attorney told me. Following him to one of the back rooms, I was surprised as hell to see Scorpio's ass sitting at one of the tables. My face immediately frowned up.

"What's up, nigga?" he asked and stood when I was completely inside the room.

"Sup Scorpio? Fuck you been up to?" I replied, even though I was mad as hell at his ass.

Scorpio was the nigga in these streets. I'd worked for him ever since I dropped out of school when I was sixteen. You would've thought the nigga would've had the decency to help me out with this lil' situation I was in, but he turned his back on me the moment I was arrested. That's why I was looking crazy as fuck when I first locked eyes with him.

"First off, you know I don't tolerate disrespect. The fact that you're looking at me like you're ready to fight shows me that we clearly have a problem," he told me.

"You're right, we do. Why are you even here? You wasn't fuckin' with me two years ago when I got into this shit." Just like that, I'd gotten amped up.

"Step out," Scorpio ordered Mr. Latimore who instantly jumped up and ran out the room like the little bitch that he was. "Don't ever come at me like you're crazy, nigga. I run these streets," he spoke through clenched teeth.

"You don't think I know that? That's why I'm pissed the fuck off. You could've made this shit disappear, but you left me to the wolves. I thought we were better than that."

"Naw, you assumed we were better than that. Not one time did I tell you that we were cool like that. In fact, I tried to warn your ass on several occasions that you were fuckin' up and you didn't want to hear that shit. You were becoming too flashy, you kept getting into fights with niggas for no reason, and you kept pissing off these random ass women. That was shit you did to yourself when I told you not to bring that much attention to yourself because then you'd be bringing attention to me and what I had going on. You think I wanted to be looking over my back for a punk ass nigga that acted like he couldn't follow directions? I'd be dumb as hell to help you out so that you could get out and revert back to the same old shit and end up getting my shit shut down. I'm not going down for no damn body. Like I told you from day one, if it ever came down to it being me or you, it's going to be your ass going down every time," he reminded me.

"That's bullshit and you know it. It's all good though because I know they don't have shit on me. This shit was consensual. I'll be out and ready to work in no time." Yeah, there was a lot of anger and resentment in my heart when it came to Scorpio's ass, but like I said, he was the man in the streets. I had to work if I wanted to eat.

"You not coming back to work for me. That's the only reason I came in here today."

"What the fuck you mean? I've always worked for you. How am I supposed to make money when I get out of here?"

"Don't know and I frankly don't give a fuck. That's not my business to worry about. When you get your ass on that stand, you better not mention me, my organization, or anyone that's associated with me." He walked up on me and the tightness in his face was evident. He was not someone I wanted or needed to piss off, but he was pushing me.

"Fuck you then, Scorpio. You could've sent somebody in here to tell me that. You didn't have to show up and ruin my fuckin' day," I told him. I wasn't even sure what he showed his face for anyway because he never did his own dirty work. Shit was crazy. It was almost as if he was purposely trying to fuck with me.

"You can't fuck me nigga, but I'm going to enjoy fuckin' your bitch." If my hands were free, I would've knocked the smirk off his face.

"Come on, Javi," Mr. Latimore stepped back in the room and said. "They are ready for us in the courtroom," he informed me.

"You better stay away from my bitch or you will be seeing me very soon," I threatened. That wasn't the best move, but Scorpio needed to know that Mignon was off limits. If he no longer fucked with me, that was cool. However, he needed to know that stickin' his dick in my bitch was not an option.

Chapter Four:

Mignon

"All rise," the bailiff stated as the judge entered the courtroom. It wasn't long after he came in that Javi was brought in with those same shackles all over his body. I'm not sure why they had to do that to him because it wasn't like he was a damn flight risk.

"You may be seated," the judge told us after a while of standing.

"May we approach the bench?" Mr. Latimore asked. The judge waved for him and the other attorney to step up. Javi turned around and allowed his eyes to roam the courtroom. Not once did he look at me. For a minute, I thought he couldn't see me until I allowed my eyes to follow his to see what he could've been searching for. It wasn't until his eyes stopped moving that I was able to zoom in on her. What I meant by her was that he was glaring at the same woman that had her ass sitting in his face keking (laughing) and shit when I stepped back inside the visitation room a few weeks back. What the hell was she even doing here?

"Javi?" I called his name. That was the only time he looked at me and gave off a slight smile.

"Hey Mignon," he dryly spoke.

"That's all you got to say to me?" I squealed. The clown ass nigga had the nerve to put a finger up to his lips to shush me. He had me so fucked up that I stood to leave out of the courtroom. One of the court officials tried to stop me but I told them that I had to go to the restroom real bad.

Outside the courtroom, I found myself pacing back and forth. I was punching my left palm with my right fist. That's how angry I was. For me to be doing that said a lot because I was not a violent person at all. It took a lot to push me over the edge and Javi knew that.

"Calm down, lil momma. It's not that serious," a deep voice said to me. It sounded like Rick Ross was talking to me and I could feel myself instantly becoming wet.

Slowly, I turned around to see who was speaking to me. I knew who he was because Javi had pointed him out to me before, but that was all I knew. Ask me what his name was, and I couldn't tell you. All I knew was that he was the one that put Javi on and helped him in ways that no one in his family had ever attempted to help him.

"Do I know you?" I asked, playing dumb.

"Baby, everybody knows who I am," he replied, licking his lips. I could've fainted like a hoe in church because everything about him caused my body to react in a way that it shouldn't have. I was with Javi, a man that worked for him, there was no way I should've been lusting over this man.

"Well, I don't, so you have a nice day." I turned to walk away from him, but I couldn't. There were men standing behind me that had me blocked in. "What the hell!" I exclaimed.

"Where you going? Turn around and talk to a nigga when you're being spoken to," he ordered.

"I don't know what women you're used to dealing with, but that ain't me. I'm not even sure why you're standing in my face right now because I have a whole nigga."

"You mean the one that's been locked away for the past two years? Yeah, I know that pussy tight and right," he announced, licking his lips again.

One thing I couldn't do was lie and say that his ass wasn't fine because he was. He reminded me of Lance Gross. He had to be about six feet and three inches tall with a muscular frame. Everything about this man was gorgeous to me.

Out of nowhere, he walked up on me. Him breathing down on my neck caused my breathing to pick up.

"I know you know my name's Scorpio and that your nigga used to work for me."

"Used to?" I quizzed, wondering what he was talking about.

"Used to. I didn't stutter. That's not what I came to you about though," he mentioned.

"Then what do you want from me? I'm not no hoe and I'm not working no streets," I fussed, assuming he was about to try to make me work for him.

"If you'd shut up long enough to listen, you'd know that I wasn't coming to you to work for me. I mean a nigga wouldn't mind you being a hoe, but that's only in the bedroom on my dick," he admitted. He walked a little closer to me. He was so close that the hairs on the back of my neck stood up. "I've been watching you for a while.

It's time for you to leave that chump alone and get on a winning team. All that shit you did for him was uncalled for. Let me show you what you're worth and what you deserve."

My thoughts were all over the place. I wanted to say something to him, but there was no point in doing so. It was clear he'd made up in his mind that he wanted me to be a part of his life but that wasn't what I wanted. Turning around, I was going to walk away from him, but the same men from earlier were still standing behind me.

"You might as well give up trying to run because what Scorpio wants, Scorpio gets," he told me.

"There's a first time for everything, Scorpio and this is going to be your first time not getting what you want because I'm not going. Now, have these large sacks of potatoes get out of my way so I can get back in the courtroom where my man is," I demanded.

Scorpio snapped his fingers and the men moved. I faced him about to thank him for being the bigger person until I saw the huge smirk on his face. Changing my mind, I twisted my ass right back inside the courtroom and took a seat next to Robin.

"You good?" she asked me as soon as I sat back down. Instead of answering her, I nodded my head, "yes."

The queasy feeling in my stomach returned. I wasn't sure what was about to happen, but whatever it was, wasn't going to be good at all.

Chapter Five:

Javi

The whole time I was in the court, my mind was on the bullshit Scorpio had said. He'd never came at me wrong before, so it had me wondering what type of shit he was on. Thoughts of him being inside of Mignon kept racing through my mind. If I could break free and grab a gun, I'd shoot his ass right between the eyes.

Mr. Latimore's punk ass asked to approach the bench. He never told me what he wanted to approach for, so it caught me off guard.

"What's up?" I asked when he came back to the table.

"Hang tight," he told me. I hated when mufuckas did that shit. Don't blindside me. If some shit was about to pop off, then I needed to know what it was in advance.

"Due to some new developments, we have no choice but to drop all charges against the defendant." That was all I remembered the judge saying. Everything else went in one ear and out the other. I didn't even care enough to find out what the new developments were. All I knew was that I was about to be a free man. Anything else didn't mean shit to me.

Standing from the table, I was in complete and utter shock. I didn't know what the hell was going on, but I wasn't going to complain. A nigga was a free man. I couldn't wait to get out of here so I can go lay-up with my woman.

"Come here, baby. I'm so glad this is over," Mignon stated. She started making her way towards me but was pushed out of the way by Shawnte.

Shawnte wrapped her arms around my neck and pulled me in for a big kiss. It was hard going so long without even being able to touch her. That time had come to an end and I was more than ready to go home and fuck the shit out of her.

"What the fuck is going on?" Mignon yelled. She came running up behind Shawnte and started swinging, but Robin caught her and pulled her back.

"Stop it, Mignon. I told you to leave his ass alone a long time ago. He's not worth your tears and he damn sure isn't worth you going to jail," Robin commented.

"Fuck you, Robin. I was the best thing that ever happened to him," Mignon acknowledged.

"Bitch, I know that. Now let him feel the shit. He thinks the grass is greener on the other side, but watch his ass come crawling back to you," she advised Mignon.

"Crawling back? To her? No ma'am. He's mine now and he won't ever look at another bitch again. I can assure you of that. By the way, thanks for helping take care of me and our son," Shawnte boasted.

Bow...

Before anyone could stop her, Mignon sent a right hook to Shawnte's jaw. Her mouth flew open and spit went flying out. My mouth dropped as a guard neared me. The fact that I was about to be released told me that I didn't need any more problems. The first thing that I did, and they'd be ready to throw my ass up under the jail. I threw my hands up in defeat because I knew that if Mignon hit me, I was going to shake the shit out of her, that was if I didn't knock her damn teeth down her throat first. Now, don't get me wrong, hitting women was not my thing. However, I felt that if they were man enough to pass a lick, they should be man enough to take one back. Mignon knew that about me so for her to even act like she wanted to try me was an issue in itself.

"Get back, Mignon. Don't come over here with that bullshit," I ordered. She kept coming. That let me know exactly how mad she really was. The calm, cool, and collected Mignon would never do anything that could cause her to end up with a record. This new Mignon was someone I didn't recognize.

When she was up on me, I could feel the sweat beads forming on my forehead. For some reason, I'd gotten nervous as hell. Why the hell hadn't the police already grabbed her ass and put her in the fuckin' handcuffs? She had already caused a scene and she was fighting in a federal building. What kind of bullshit was that?

"You know you don't have any money. Think about what you're doing. I'd hate for you to be sitting in jail because you don't have anybody to get you out," I reminded her.

"You a lie. I'll sell pussy before I let my bestie bitch sit in jail behind a no good as nigga," Robin hollered.

My eyes briefly left Mignon and landed on Robin. That gave Mignon the chance to catch me off guard because within seconds, she lifted her knee and struck me between the legs. I immediately dropped down to my knees. The pain running through my body was excruciating. There was nothing I could do to her because I was too busy rolling around on the floor trying to mask the pain. Shawnte was going to be one mad bitch tonight because if my shit didn't stop hurting anytime soon, there was no way she was going to be able to get any of this "fresh out the pin dick" tonight.

Chapter Six:

Mignon

Robin tried to grab me and pull me out of the courtroom, but it was too late. The officers had grabbed my ass up and threw me in handcuffs. The shit was embarrassing as hell. There was no way I could get myself out of jail because I'd been using all of my money to take care of his ass. Robin depended on the niggas she dealt with to take care of her, so I was fucked.

My head dropped as I was being escorted out of the courtroom and over to the police station. How was I going to be able to explain to my mother that I was in jail? I'm sure my father was turning flips in his casket right now. Damn! I should've walked away when Robin told me to, but I couldn't. Her telling me that they had a child really fucked with me. Especially, since the two times I'd gotten pregnant by his ass, he made me abort my babies saying we weren't ready. The thought of that alone was enough for me to want to fight his ass.

"Let me go. Let me fuck him up. If I'm going to catch a charge, I'm going to have a damn good reason for catching it." I fought with the officers as much as I could trying to break free and as soon as I saw that I had an audience.

All I could think about was wrapping my hands around Javi's neck for the way he'd done me. All the time I wasted out of my life working to save for his punk ass and the whole time he was taking my money and sending it to his make-believe ass family.

"Calm down before I charge you with resisting arrest and obstruction of justice. Shit, we can charge you with a list of shit," one of the officers told me.

"Yeah. You gonna kill my black ass too or have you realized that Black Lives Matter?" I sarcastically asked, being a smart ass.

"Cut the bullshit. We arrested you because you did something to be arrested. We aren't going to rape you, beat you, kill you, or none of that other bullshit. This is a legit ass arrest and I'm not losing my job over no damn body."

As soon as those words left his mouth, I started laughing. I thought back to the video where the black woman was apprehended by a police officer and started dancing and singing, "You about to lose your job." That shit was funny as hell. What I was going through wasn't funny, but I needed that laugh in that moment.

"You about to lose your job. You about to lose your job." I started singing and dancing as they walked me inside the police station. The cop that was arguing with me about not hurting me started laughing.

"Your ass is crazy as fuck for real," he told me and dropped his head. I knew he was trying his best to keep a straight face, but it was hard. Hell, even his partner was laughing.

When we got inside the police station, they wasted no time putting my information in the computer and fingerprinting me. Never in a million years would you have paid me to believe I would have a damn mugshot.

"Can I get my phone call?" I asked.

"No, you can't get anything right now. We are going to put you in a cell so you can think about what you've done," the officer told me and chuckled. They took me to a holding cell and walked away.

The little time that I sat in there, the only thing I thought about was who I was going to call. Calling my parents was out of the question because I felt like all they were going to do was judge me. I fucked up and I knew I fucked up bad. My whole family told me time and time again to leave Javi's ass alone and I was too stubborn to do it. Now, I knew why they didn't like me. They were right by telling me that I deserved better. If only I would've believed it for myself then I wouldn't be in the situation I was in now.

It seemed like I'd been in that holding cell forever, but I don't even think a whole hour passed before I was told I was free to go. That was music to my ears. Luckily it didn't take me as long to leave as it did for me to get booked.

Chapter Seven:

Scorpio

My eyes stayed glued on Mignon as she sashayed away from me. Her hips swayed from side to side. Everything about her was perfect to me.

Normally, I wasn't the type of nigga that fucked with another nigga's bitch. I wasn't even the type that went after a woman. They always flocked to me. I'd bumped into Mignon on several occasions and not once did she pay me any attention. That let me know that she was loyal. Then when I had the small conversation with her today and she confirmed that she had a man, I clearly saw how she held him down. There were plenty of women that said they'll be by your side while you're going through some shit but when it started to get hard, they ran. Mignon didn't do that. She was a real ride or die for Javi's dumb ass and he fucked it up. That was fine by me because I had no problem showing him how to treat a woman of her caliber.

"You just going to let her walk away from you like that, man?" Twist asked me.

Twist was my right-hand man. We'd been kicking it hard for the past ten years. It's crazy because when we first met, it was during the time that my parents had kicked me out the house. I learned that my father was cheating on my mother, yet she allowed him to stick around. That pissed me off because I knew she deserved better. You can't make a person get better if they don't want it for themselves, right? Mother or not, I wasn't about to kiss her ass just to get her to open her eyes.

My father and I got into it when he came in and heard me telling her that she needed to leave him. This was after learning that he'd had an outside child on her. Hell, I seemed to be angrier about the situation than she was. Come to find out, my mother knew about the shit for a while. She was just playing dumb in front of me in order to save face. So, yeah, a nigga snapped and was asked to leave. They didn't have to tell me twice. I grabbed my shit and hit the streets. I worked my ass off to build the empire that I had today.

Twist was the nigga that I learned was my father's outside child. I couldn't stand his ass when I found out who he was and tried to kill him a few times. I was young and dumb and didn't know what I was doing so I failed epically at that. It took for me to realize that he didn't do anything wrong for me to kill the beef that I had towards him. To make a long story short, we linked up and realized we had more in common than I thought, and we've been tighter than braids freshly done by the Africans, since then.

"Shut up, nigga. You know this shit temporary," I replied.

"It may be, but it's still funny as shit. I don't think I've ever seen a bitch turn you down," he noted.

"Exactly! That's how I know it's temporary. She'll be mine by the end of the month. Bet that."

"The end of the month? Nigga, I thought you were going to say by the end of the day."

"Naw. She delicate. Plus, she bout to get her heart broken. A nigga gonna swoop in and make that shit right. Just wait... Besides, I don't want her jumping to be with me because this ditzy ass nigga bout to fuck her over. She needs to know what she's about to get herself into when she fucks with a nigga like me," I told him.

"I heard that shit."

Twist and I sat quietly in the back of my blacked out Suburban, watching all the shit play out in the courtroom. I had one of my workers go in with a tie that had a camera attached to it so I could see everything that went down.

"Damn, I can't believe you got those charges dropped like that," Twist stated.

"I wasn't going to, but I had to. I needed that nigga to be out so that the shit with him and Shawnte could come to the light," I told him and chuckled.

"Damn nigga, I see how you did that. When they shit was out there, Shawty would be free to get away from his ass," he commented.

"Exactly! That leaves the door open for me."

"I don't get it though. Why the hell would you not just go after her while he was away? You had every opportunity to and you always get what you want."

"It wasn't the right time. I had to make sure I had some shit together with me, so I knew I'd be ready to be the man she was going to need me to be and the man that she deserved. Look, you worry about you. I got all this shit over here on lock," I responded causing us both to laugh.

As Mignon was being carried out the court, I never moved. I waited until they told me that she was booked before I called my attorney to get all that shit dropped. My attorney was so damn good that he had the shit wiped out the system within a matter of minutes. It was as if she were never even arrested.

"You need a ride?" I asked her when she walked outside of the police station. Her face was covered in dried up mascara. I'm sure it was from all the crying she'd apparently been doing.

"No. I have a car," she snapped.

"Don't get snappy with me. If it weren't for me, your ass would probably still be sitting behind bars," I rebutted.

"I didn't ask you for a damn thing so don't come running over here like I'm about to bust it open and give you some pussy for helping me out. Shit, you probably knew about Javi and his bitch when you ran into me earlier."

Hearing her say that caused my head to drop. That had to be the first time in a long time that I allowed someone to talk to me like that or make me feel bad.

"You did know, huh? Why the fuck didn't you just tell me what it was? Let me guess, you were on that 'bro code' shit so you had no choice but to allow me to sit in that damn courtroom like a fuckin' fool."

"Bro code? What the fuck are you talking about? That nigga would have had to be a bro for me to be on some fake as bro code shit. I'm not a snitch and I damn sure don't get into other people's business, so it wasn't my place to say a damn thing."

"Oh really?"

"I said what the fuck I said."

"Well guess what, I'm saying what the fuck I got to say too. Fuck you and fuck Javi. Both of y'all *Brokeback Mountain* ass niggas better stay the fuck away from me," she spazzed and walked away.

"BITCH!" I yelled out behind her. Was it wrong for me to disrespect her? Yeah, but she disrespected me too and I'm one of those niggas that will give you what you give me.

"Damn bro, she just went straight off on your ass." Twist was falling all over the damn seat laughing at the shit. There wasn't a damn thing funny to me.

"Get me the fuck out of here," I told my driver when I slide back in my SUV.

"What you gonna do now?" Twist asked.

"Fuck that bitch! Aye, take me to see Sierra, I need my damn dick sucked."

The driver cranked up and pulled away from the curb. Shit was crazy as hell. The way that Mignon handled me pissed me off and turned me on at the same damn time. Her ass didn't know it yet, but she was mine.

Chapter Eight:

Mignon

(Two Weeks Later...)

It had been a few weeks since everything happened at the court. My mind pondered a lot over what happened and how I got to where I was.

Robin had come over to help me finally pack up Javi's shit. Anything that I purchased, I kept and anything that still had the tags on, I returned to the store. I wasn't going to get something out of my heartbreak one way or another. I hadn't even been to work because I hadn't been able to go past two hours without thinking about everything and crying. Luckily, I'd worked so much during these past two years that I had enough vacation time to take off work and still get paid. Trust me, I couldn't afford to pass up any coins at this point.

"You good girl?" Robin asked, removing me from my thoughts.

"No bitch. I don't understand why he would do that to me," I cried. Right as I broke down, I spotted Javi's toothbrush. "Do you have to shit?" I asked Robin.

"Ewwww... Bitch no. I did it before I walked over here." She fell out laughing. I threw my index finger up and waltzed inside the bathroom.

Grabbing his toothbrush, I rubbed the bristles around in the toilet, on the floor, and under the sole of my shoe before I placed it back in the toothbrush holder and threw it inside of his duffle bag.

Little by little, we started dragging his stuff out of the house and placing it by the mailbox. That was so his ass wouldn't have to come fucking with me. Just grab his shit and go. That was the way it needed to be and the way I was going to make sure it was. Surely, it was going to kill him that I wasn't trying to kiss his ass to be with him again. His ass was undeserving of me any damn ways.

"You okay, sis?" Robin asked once we'd flopped down on my couch.

"I'm as good as I'm going to be. I can't believe he did this to me. Aren't I good enough to be loved?" That was something I always found myself doing since I was hurt; questioning myself as a woman.

"Bitch don't let me hear you ask no stupid shit like that again. He's a man and a man is going to do what he's going to do. No, I'm not saying all men are like that, but Javi was a punk ass nigga. He didn't deserve you. Consider this as God removing him from your life to make room for the man that actually belongs in your life and in your heart."

Everything she was saying sounded good, but it didn't take away from the hurt I was feeling.

Bam...Bam... Bam...

"Who the fuck is that?" I asked as someone continuously beat on my door.

"Who the hell you think it is? You know damn well it ain't nobody but Javi's retarded ass."

"I don't know why when we already put all his shit out the door."

Taking a deep breath, I headed towards the front door. Swinging it open, I allowed my hands to rest on my hips as I prepared myself for the bullshit he was about to hit me with.

"Where the fuck is the rest of my shit?"

"What shit? Everything that belonged to you is over there," I told him, pointing to the pile of shit I'd neatly stacked for him by the mailbox. "Get your shit and leave. There's nothing else here for you."

"That's not all of my shit. Where my game?" he quizzed.

"My bad. I meant to say everything that belonged to you that you paid for is right over there," I corrected myself.

"Bit-" Javi raised his hand to hit me but it was caught in mid-air. We were both shocked as hell to turn around and find Scorpio standing there.

Chapter Nine:

Javi

"What the fuck?"

"I know you wasn't about to hit my girl."

"Your girl?" Mignon and I both said in unison. Where the fuck had this lump head nigga come from and where the hell did he get off thinking it was cool for him to fuck with my ex bitch? Regardless to whether I was still with her or not, she was off limits to him or any of the other niggas that I used to consider to be my homeboys.

"You heard what the fuck I said. Now, take yo shit and get the fuck on before I have to make some noise out here."

"I don't want no trouble, Javi. Just leave." The fact that Mignon was taking this nigga's side infuriated me. She didn't even know his ass. At least, I thought she didn't.

"Hol' the fuck up. You been fuckin' this nigga? You gave this nigga my pussy?" I chided.

"You gave that bitch my dick?" she rebutted. That caught me off guard. Mignon was never the type of chick that came out of pocket with me. She was always so mild and timid which is why I did what I did to her.

"This my last time telling you to leave before I air this bitch out."

"Come on, baby. I'll get you another game," Shawnte came over and told me. We both knew that was a lie because the bitch didn't have shit. She'd been living off the money Mignon was sending me to pay Mr. Latimore's ass.

Shawnte grabbed my hand and led me away from Mignon's house. We loaded my stuff up in the back of her 2001 Honda Accord and slid inside. It took her trying to crank the car five times before it finally started.

Pow...

The sound of a gun going off caused me to duck down in my seat. I looked up and her ass was sitting there laughing and shit.

"What the fuck are you doing? Get down!" I demanded. "You didn't hear that gunshot?" I exclaimed. Deep down, I felt like Mignon sent Scorpio outside to kill me.

"Baby, get up," Shawnte calmly directed.

"No. Either you need to drive this bitch or get the fuck down," I erratically ordered.

"Nigga get your scary ass up. That was just my car backfiring. It does that from time to time," she explained.

It took a few minutes before I finally slid back up into my seat. She was falling over laughing at me and shit. It was embarrassing as hell, but I'd rather be scared than dead.

"Come on so you can take me to get my new game since you doing all that laughing and shit."

"With what money? You know she stopped funding us and I don't work."

"I thought I told you to save some of that money for when I got out. That was supposed to help us out until we were able to get on our feet."

"I had bills, what did you expect me to do... Work?"

"Are you even being serious right now? You think you too good to work?"

"Hell yeah. You've been taking care of me ever since we met. You need to keep that up. Especially, since we been talking about getting married."

Hearing her remind me of what I said while I was deep inside of her caused me to cringe. In no way was I going to marry her. She was lazy. She didn't like to cook or clean. Of course, it took for me to walk away from Mignon and to move in with Shawnte to figure that out. It was sad how niggas always thought they were getting something better than what they had and nine times out of ten, we were getting shit.

"You cooking today or no?" I asked. She at least got food stamps, so there was no reason she couldn't cook. I was tired of eating hot dogs, noodles, and tv dinners.

"I just got my nails done. You know I'm not about to be in no kitchen trying to cook or wash dishes. You too damn demanding for me. I liked you better when we lived separately," she acknowledged.

"Don't worry, I feel the same way. Wait until I get on my feet and we won't have to worry about this little situation anymore," I told her. I meant that shit. Just as soon as I got with her, I was ready to get rid of her. It had me wondering if I'd really fucked up enough to not be able to get Mignon back.

"What is that supposed to mean?"

"Absolutely nothing. Pull over at this Popeyes," I told her.

After rolling her eyes and smacking her lips a few times, she finally pulled into the parking lot.

"Stay in the car," I directed as I reached under the seat.

"I'm glad you grabbed your wallet," she said while I was putting something in my pocket. I shook my head and got out of the car without responding. I was seriously tired of her ass.

There were four people standing inside Popeyes besides the workers. I stood back and waited for all of them to order, acting as if I didn't know what I wanted. Then when the last person got their food, I walked up to the counter.

"Welcome to Popeyes, would you like to try our chicken sandwich?" the cashier asked me.

"Naw. Let me get three of those $23.99 family meal deals," I stated.

"Would you like that dark or white?"

"Mixed."

"Mild or spicy?"

"Mixed."

"What's your sides for the first one?"

"Give me two red beans and rice, two Cajun rices, and two mashed potatoes. One with gravy and one without."

The girl put my order in and told me that my total was $77.74. I patted my pocket down like I was searching for my wallet while she walked away to prepare the food. She came back a short while later and put the food on the counter. That was shocking to me because Popeyes never moved that damn fast, but I wasn't complaining. My goal was to be in and out of there and that's what I was about to do.

Picking up a napkin from the register, I asked the woman if she had a pen. She looked at me and smiled. I'm sure that was because she thought I was about to either give her my phone number or ask for hers, but it wasn't that type of party. Shawnte had worked my damn nerves so much since I'd been home that I really wasn't in the mood to be bothered with no other female; unless it was Mignon.

Carefully, I pushed the napkin over to her. She glanced down at it and peered back up at me. The smile that once appeared on her face had slowly faded away. I tapped my waist, so she'd know I wasn't playing with her. She looked around like she wanted to scream for help, but I nodded to my damn chicken. She quickly pushed the bag towards me and ducked down. I grabbed the food and hauled ass out of the restaurant.

"Go... Go... Go..." I hollered at Shawnte as I jumped back inside the car. Thankfully she'd left it running so I didn't have to worry about the bitch not moving and us getting caught.

"What happened?" she questioned me.

"Stop being fuckin' nosey and just drive damnit." She looked at me like she was about to say something but did the right thing by keeping her fuckin' mouth shut.

The situation with Mignon and Scorpio plagued my mind. It was something that was going to bother me until I put an end to whatever the hell they could possibly have going on. The one thing that wasn't going to worry me was wondering what I was going to eat over the next few days. I didn't give a damn if I turned into a chicken, my ass was going to be good and full.

Chapter Ten:

Scorpio

"What are you doing here?" Mignon asked when Javi was out of earshot.

"I came to see my lady," I advised her.

"Damn bitch. You didn't tell me you were fuckin' with his fine ass. Where you get him from?" her friend asked.

"Back up, Shawty. I'm fuckin' with your girl. Don't refer to me as fine and be lustin' all over me and shit like my woman not standing right there," I told her. I didn't play that unloyal shit and I could tell that if I tossed my dick out there to her friend, that bitch would swallow my shit whole.

"Would you stop calling me your lady because you aren't my man. I'm not dealing with any more of you so-called thugs."

"So-called? Baby, I'm the man in these streets. You need to find somebody else to play with."

"That's a good idea. I think I do need to find somebody else to play with. Now, thank you for getting Javi to leave. You can leave as well," Mignon commented. She turned to walk away from me once again and I grabbed her away. "What the fu-" She caught herself from whatever she was about to say when she looked up and saw the look in my eyes.

"Leave!" I told her friend.

"What? I'm not leaving my girl here with you and you over here grabbing her like you own her. Let her go before I call the cops."

"Tell her to leave before I make her leave," I asserted. Mignon's eyes locked with mine and she just stared at me. It was as if we were in a trance.

"It's okay, Robin. I got this. You can leave," Mignon told her.

"Are you serious?" Robin quizzed. She rubbed the top of her head as if she were confused with what was going on. I didn't blame her. If a nigga I'd never met just came out of the woodworks, barking out orders, I'd be concerned too. I probably wouldn't even leave. She wasn't me though.

"Yes, I'm going to be okay," Mignon assured her.

"Fine, but if he fucks you up or something, don't call me."

"Baby girl, I don't beat up women unless I'm beating up their pussy, which is exactly what I'm about to do with your girl. Take your bitter ass on somewhere," I fumed, tired of hearing her mouth.

"You going to let him talk to me like that?" Robin popped her lips and crossed her arms over her chest. I finally let Mignon go and turned to face Robin.

"You know what, I'm not even about to do this with you." I was really about to put her in her place, but I stopped. I threw my hand up and motioned for someone to come towards me. Twist hopped out the truck and made his way over to where we were.

"What's up, bro?" he asked. He had his hand on his hip where he kept his pistol, locked and loaded. I knew that was because he was ready to handle business.

"It's not even that serious, bro. Do something with lil momma here," I told him.

Without hesitation, Twist threw Robin over his shoulder and headed towards the SUV with her. Naturally, she was kicking and screaming. We weren't worried about anybody calling the police because we ran those streets. Even if they did, I had so many of them on my payroll that this shit wouldn't even be logged in to the dispatch system.

"Hey! Put her down," Mignon yelled. I placed my hand over her mouth and pushed her inside her house. Shutting the door with my foot, I kept pushing her back until we were in her bedroom.

"So, you gonna rape me?" she asked as soon as I moved my hand away from her mouth.

"Take your clothes off," I demanded.

"What? I'm not doing shit," she fussed. "You need to leave."

"Take off your fuckin' clothes, NOW!" I barked. She looked at me with fear in her eyes. It saddened me that she'd think I'd really hurt her, but I didn't say anything. I kept going with what I was there to do.

Taking her time, she removed each article of clothing that she had on. I admired every inch of her body. From the moment I laid eyes on her, I only imagined what she would look like underneath her clothes. I'd never seen anything so beautiful in my life.

Mignon wasn't that skinny chick that most men went for. You know the small model like body with long fake hair and shit. She was beyond all of that. If you've ever seen the model Toccara Jones then you've seen Mignon. She was the true definition of curvalicious with her coffee colored skin tone, nice perky breast, onion shaped ass, flat stomach, toned body, and a smile that could light up any room. She wore her hair in a bob that fit her face perfectly. She had to be a size 14/16 which was perfect for me. Then the fact that she was bow-legged as fuck did something to me. The thought of her legs alone always had my dick on go. Mignon was bad as fuck and that was something I don't think she realized. If she did, she wouldn't have stayed with Javi and put up with his bullshit for as long as she did.

"Lay down on your stomach." As I was giving her directions, my tone calmed, and I noticed the tension that was once in her body was no longer there. With her lying on the bed, I pulled a bandana out of my pocket and placed it over her eyes so she couldn't see.

Taking my phone out of my pocket, I sent out a text as I continued to talk to her. She tried to play hard with me by not responding to anything I said to her but when I got to talking about how much I thought she deserved, she began talking back.

"What's that sound?" she asked, referring to the movement that was going on in the room.

"Trust me," I told her.

"Trust you? You think I can trust you after all the shit you pulled today?"

"Mignon, we were doing good. Don't lose sight of what I'm trying to do here."

"What are you trying to do? Be a perv! Who makes someone that keeps telling them to leave them alone, take their clothes off?" She kept ranting and raving, and it had started to piss me off. One thing I couldn't stand was a bitch that nagged and she was starting to show me that side of her. That was something I was going to have to break before I even thought about taking things a step further with her. She was doing too much and I didn't have time for any unnecessary drama in my life.

"You got this boss man," I said to someone as I stood to leave. "Enjoy," I glanced back at her once more before exiting her home.

The SUV was moving back and forth when I got out there to it. I reached for my gun because I figured some foul shit was going on. What the hell could be going on inside that had my shit rocking like that? Looking around, I could see the driver standing on side of the SUV laughing.

"What the fuck is going on?" I asked him. He wasn't concerned at all.

"That's your boy," he said. That had me thinking Twist was in my shit wilding out. I snatched the door open and damn near fell out when I saw how he had Robin's ass bent up like a pretzel. He was fuckin' the shit out of her ass. I shut the damn door and shook my head.

"Call me another car. Ain't no way in the hell I'm getting in this bitch until it's cleaned out," I chuckled.

It wasn't long before someone else pulled up to grab me. I told them to take me straight to my crib. For the life of me, I couldn't wrap my mind around what was up with Mignon. She was making me chase her ass like I was the police and being paid for the shit. Yeah, I wanted her true enough, but was it really worth this big ass headache?

Chapter Eleven:

Mignon

The feeling of something wet dripping down my back almost caused me to jump off the bed until I felt some warm hands touching me. They started rubbing all over my body giving me a massage. That was something I'd never had before. It was something that I could never afford and Javi's ass wasn't doing shit unless it would end up with him benefiting from it.

"I'm sorry," I told Scorpio. "I didn't mean to be so harsh with you. I just thought that you were about to rape me or something when you told me to take my clothes off. You could've just told me what you wanted, and I wouldn't have been so resistant," I said.

Waiting for him to reply, I was shocked when he didn't say anything. He didn't take me as the type that would keep their mouth shut. Besides, I was apologizing to him. It was rude as hell for him to not even acknowledge that I was talking to him.

Snatching the blindfold off, I was even more shocked to find that his ass had left. There were candles lit all over the room. Shit, I was so consumed with wanting to fuss at him that I didn't pay attention to the soft music that was playing in the background.

"Bitcccchhhh..." I heard Robin squeal from the living room. Quickly, I jumped up and pulled the sheet over my body. "Oh well damn, I guess somebody else was getting their needs met too," she said and started twerking in the doorway.

"Bitch, no ma'am. Scorpio had this set up so I could get a massage," I explained to her.

"Wait... you mean to tell me that you didn't give him any pussy and he still did this for you?"

"No, I didn't give him any pussy. He didn't deserve any. Not after the way he's been talking to me like he's my daddy or something."

"Shittin' me."

"Yeah, I know I'm shittin' you. All he had to do was make eye contact with your ass and you would've dropped your panties. I'm surprised you didn't fuck his friend," I stated, giving her the side-eye. The smirk that appeared across her face showed how wrong I was. "Damn bitch, you couldn't have waited a day?"

"My pussy was purring, and he had the meat to feed eat. Fuck I look like passing on meals?" she joked. I couldn't help but laugh because she was retarded as hell. "Seriously though, Mignon, you really need to stop being so hard on Scorpio. That man can have any chick that he wants but he's chasing you. That says a lot. Stop letting the hurt that Javi caused you make you miss out on something that could be so good for you," Robin confidently spoke.

"I hear ya. It's only been a few weeks, Robin. I need some time to heal from all this shit. I will, however, tell Scorpio thank you for being so nice to me. If he wants to see where things can go in the future, that's one thing. Right now, I can't do anything but have conversation with him; if I can do that."

"That's better than nothing. Now, let's get dressed. We're going out. I'm tired of you mopping around here when you should be out living your best life. We too young to be staying in the house all the time."

Robin was right. All I'd done was work and come home to wait on Javi's calls when he was away. He took away the best years of my life. There was no coming back from that. What he did to me was fucked all the way up. Now, I was damaged goods. No matter what man came to me, I was going to be scared to give him a chance all because I was scorned by Javi's wannabe thug's ass.

"You game, girl?" she asked.

"Do I really have a choice?" I responded.

"You always have a choice. I'm not going to make you do anything you don't want to do. If you decide that you don't want to go, then don't expect me to sit around looking crazy with you." I felt like she was giving me an ultimatum. Although, I'm sure that's not what her intentions were. "You down to go have a good time?"

"Yeah. Let's do it," I replied.

"Okay. Let me run home and get a little nap in and we can head out around 9," she commented.

Robin didn't give me the chance to respond before she jumped up and exited the house. I allowed my body to fall back on the bed. All I could think about was all the stuff Robin had said to me. She was right. There was no reason in hell for me to be walking around looking sad when Javi was walking around without a care in the damn world. He was living his best life. Why shouldn't I?

As I laid in the bed, I thought about what I could wear. It had been so long since I'd been out that I wasn't sure if I even had anything to wear. It would be nice if I would've had enough time to go to the mall, but since I didn't, I was going to have to improvise. If push came to shove, my last resort would be to go over to Robin's and borrow something hot and sexy from her. Those were my final thoughts as I closed my eyes. Thinking about Javi tired me out. That should've been enough for me to want to let him go. It was hard. It wasn't going to happen overnight, that much I knew. When It did happen, I was going to be ready for it. That was my last thought as I allowed my sleep to consume me.

Chapter Twelve:

Scorpio

When I left Mignon's house, I got a call from Twist telling me he wanted to get out the house. After all the bad luck I'd been having lately, getting out the house sounded like a great idea.

Dressed in Versace from my head down to my feet, I grabbed my keys, phone, and wallet before locking up my house and heading out to my whip. I decided to drive so that I'd be able to leave when I was ready. That and I didn't want any more incidents like the one I had when Twist was fuckin' Mignon's friend in my shit. Ain't no way I was going to be sitting around waiting for somebody to come scoop me up when I had more than enough cars to drive on my own.

Stepping outside the door, I noticed Twist was pulling into my driveway. He parked next to my Charger and hopped out the car.

"Whaddup bro?" he asked, dapping me up.

"Not a damn thang," I replied. We chopped It up for a second before heading out.

We pulled up to Freelon's and I immediately noted the line that was wrapped around the corner. That made me want to turn around and take my black ass back home. That's exactly what I tried to do. Twist wasn't going for that.

"Where you going?" Twist asked, making his way towards me.

"Nigga, I'm not about to stand in that long ass line," I informed him.

"You must've forgotten who we are. We have more pull than anyone else around this bitch," Twist reminded me. A small smirk appeared on my face as I thought about what he'd said. He was speaking straight facts. There wasn't shit on this earth I had to wait for. That was until I met Mignon's ass. She was giving me a run for my money. The only reason I was going for the shit was because my mother always told me that anything worth having was worth waiting for. Even though I didn't know exactly what it was, I felt like waiting for Mignon was the best thing for me.

"Sup Puncho?" Twist and I dapped up the bouncer as we neared the front door.

"I can't complain. Out here making this money," he replied.

"I heard that shit," I told him. "I done already told you when you ready to start making that big money, come pay your boy a visit," I commented to him.

"You ain't said nothing but a word," he said.

Puncho, Twist, and I stood at the front door choppin' it up. It seemed like we'd been there forever when it had only been a few minutes. After a while of listening to people complain about us standing there, I decided it was time for us to enter.

"We bout to head on in. Holla at us later, Puncho," I said and walked on in. Twist was right behind me.

Throwing the chick a few stacks that was standing at the front of the club, we made our way over to VIP. There were bad bitches everyone.

"Damn, I'm bout to get a bunch of pussy tonight," Twist shouted over the music.

"Didn't you just fuck ol' girl in my whip," I reminded him.

"Damn. There's a quota for how much pussy I can get?" he joked. I started laughing at his ass. "Don't worry, bruh. I know you going home with some pussy tonight too."

"I'm good. I got me. You just worry about what the fuck you got going on. Ass gonna fuck around and catch something."

"What you mean by that?"

"Shidddd... Nigga, you fuck with that saltwater fish. I fucks with that premium freshwater shit," I chuckled.

"Fuck you," he chided and threw me the middle finger. The shit was funny as hell, which was the reason we both fell out laughing.

As we sat down in the VIP section, all kind of women came flocking over to us, as usual. Twist stopped their ass before they could step foot in our section. The one thing I could say about him was that he made sure he scanned any chick that wanted to get down with us. We wasn't on no bullshit or drama and he made sure none of those chicks was bringing that shit our way.

"Watch back, I'm trying to get to that sexy ass nigga over there." I looked up at the sound of her voice. When I locked eyes with Aniya, a smile spread across my face.

"Let her in," I advised Twist.

"Hell no!" Twist refused. My face quickly frowned as I peered up at his ass.

"Fuck you say to me?" I chided, standing from where I was sitting.

Twist was my boy, but Aniya had been my girl for years. Well, she used to be until a nigga found out she was trying to get pregnant thinking that would make me keep her around. I didn't like that setup ass bullshit and little did she know, she was my queen. Not once did I step out on her or make another bitch feel superior to her; not even my mother. She couldn't accept that. She thought because I was in the streets then I was doing shit other than making money. That caused us our three-year relationship. To top that off, as soon as we broke up, I started hearing about how she'd been in the streets with other niggas. That was unforgivable. I was all for loyalty and she obviously wasn't.

When we first broke up, that shit did something to me. I tried my best to hide my emotions, but I couldn't. Even working in the streets more didn't help. It actually had me fuckin' up in the streets. Twist had to sit my black ass down and do his own little intervention making me realize that Aniya's fuck up was going to cause me to lose it all. Thinking about going back to the poverty-stricken lifestyle quickly snapped me out of my funk. Now that I'm back to the way I was from the jump, there was no reason for me to give her the chance to come in and disrupt that.

Aniya was bad though. She was my own Kelly Rowland with the dark chocolate skin complexion, long-slender build, with just enough ass and breast for me to cuff in my hands. She was all I ever wanted and needed, but she allowed her greed and pride to destroy what we had.

"I said No, Scorpio. You know what she did to you, and I can't see you go down that road again," he told me. He was right and we both knew it.

"I'm just speaking," I asserted, and pushed him out the way. My mouth told him I was just speaking, but my dick was ready to jump back inside of her. The place that used to be his home two or three times a day.

"Hey baby," she greeted me and pulled me in for a hug. Her touch alone did something to me. That was something I couldn't deny.

"Sup girl? How have you been?"

"I've been well. It's so good to see you. Where have you been hiding?"

"Hiding? What I got to hide for?" I chuckled. For some reason, I felt nervous. It was as if something was telling me to get away from her. When I turned around and saw Twist, I realized what that something was. He was staring a hole through my ass. "Aye, I gotta handle something. I'll get up with you later," I lied.

"I thought we could spend a little time together. I've missed you so much," she commented, moving a little closer to me. I could feel my dick stiffening in my pants, so I pushed her back.

"I'll get up with you later," I repeated. She smacked her lips and stomped away. Twist sat behind me cracking up laughing but I didn't find anything to be funny.

"I'm glad you made her leave before I had to tear this whole club up about my man," another female spoke. I didn't recognize the voice. Twist apparently knew who it was because he pushed past me to get to her.

"What's up, ma?" he asked.

"Hey baby! I thought I'd take you up on that offer from earlier," she said. That's when I thought about who he was with earlier and did a quick about face. My eyes instantly locked with Mignon. In that moment, it was like she and I were the only people in the club. I wanted to walk over to her and say something, but I didn't. Due to the way she'd been blowing me off, a nigga was in his feelings. Yes, men get in their feelings too; even thug niggas like me. So, I was not about to make this shit easy for her.

Chapter Thirteen:

Mignon

Robin came storming inside my bedroom with a bunch of clothes in her hand.

"What are you doing?" I curiously asked her. It didn't take a rocket scientist to see that she was trying to dress me up. That wasn't an issue to me. The issue was her waking me up out of my good sleep.

"You already know what I'm doing. You've been sitting around the house in a slumber for two years behind someone that wasn't worth the shit at the bottom of your shoe and now you have a chance to be with one of the top niggas in the streets and you trippin'. You got to get your shit together, girl," she lectured me.

"What you mean? I do have my shit together. Robin, I just got out of a long relationship; I'm not ready for another one."

"Mignon, you weren't in a relationship. You was holding on to something that should've been let go a very long time ago. Let's just call a spade a spade. I tried to tell you that on several occasions, but you didn't want to listen to me. Now, you have no choice. Either you're going to step your game up and find someone that's really worth your time or you're going to keep allowing that clown ass nigga, Javi, to have control over your mind, body, and heart." It wasn't like she wasn't right, but I still didn't feel ready.

"I'm not ready, Robin," I admitted.

"You don't have to jump into a relationship, but you can test the waters. You can have a conversation with someone and get to know them. What if he is really the one for you? Are you going to disappoint God while he's trying to tell you something?"

My eyes immediately got big. Robin only mentioned God when she was up to no good. The way that she was now. That girl didn't have the sense her mother gave her.

"You make me sick."

"Be quiet for a minute," she instructed. Clamping my lips together, I watched as she put a hand up to her ear.

"What are you doing?" I asked.

"Ssssshhhhhh... Just listen to God. I hear Him, you don't?"

"Bitch, all I hear is your loud ass."

"Ssssshhhhhh.... Just listen," she repeated before leaning over to my ear. *"Get that dick, bitch,"* she whispered, pretending to be. "Did you hear Him?" If only you could've seen the look on my face. I swear that girl was retarded, but I loved her crazy ass for that.

"You get on my nerves," I told her and stood from the bed. We both laughed as I tried on the outfits that she brought over to the house for me to go through.

Robin was fine as hell. She looked like the model Saleisha Showers, only she had hazel colored eyes. They were actually slanted like she was mixed with Asian. She used to get mad when people would say that to her. Now she takes it as a compliment and keeps it moving.

Sometimes I was envious of her petite frame and the fact that she always had men throwing themselves at her. Not only that, but she wasn't afraid to go after what she wanted. I'd always been so reserved and hated that about myself. Often times I questioned how we were friends when we were so different. Whatever the reason was, I was glad because I couldn't have asked for a better friend.

Robin was smaller than me, but whenever she went shopping, she would pick out clothes for both of us. She knew I'd refuse to take anything from her, so she always kept the clothes at her house. That's how she was able to bring me over clothes that I could fit. She was crazy, with a heart of gold. She had my back no matter if I was wrong or right. She'd defended me in public and corrected me in private. She kept everything a buck with me and she stayed on my ass when I was in the wrong. I couldn't have asked for a better friend.

After going through several outfits, I decided to go with this red Go-Go like dress that only had one sleeve. On the side that was sleeveless, there were spaces that showed my skin. It stopped right below my ass. That was something that I normally wouldn't wear. The fact that it looked good on me and I actually thought about what Robin said is what prompted me to wear it. She tried to get me to put some heels on with it. I told her hell no behind that. The way that we were dressed let me know that we were heading to some club and I was not about to have my damn feet hurting and my heels leaning in like the London Bridge from trying to dance in heels, so I decided on a cute pair of wedges that were black and red and had the little rhinestones on it that was similar to the ones on my dress.

"My chick bad, my chick hood. My chick do stuff that your chick wish she could." Robin started twerking as she rapped out the words to *My Chick Bad* by Ludacris. Yeah, I started dancing with her because I was feeling bad as hell the way I was dressed. It was new to me but the way it had me feeling let me know that I'd be doing it again.

We checked ourselves in the mirror to make sure we looked good before locking up and leaving my house. Of course, Robin tricked me into driving because she claimed she was planning to get wasted tonight. That was something that I wasn't going to do because I had to be aware of my surroundings at all times. My paranoia was not set up for me to even be in a large crowd like the one we were about to step into, so this was big for me. There was no way I was going to be off my game being somewhere I wasn't familiar with.

Pulling up to the front of the club, I saw that the line was wrapped around the corner. That let me know that the club was on point. It also let me know that I did good by not wearing heels.

"Come on girl," Robin told me.

"I have to park," I replied.

"You don't see that valet? Girl, get out of this car and quit trying to find a reason to dip out on me." She knew me well. My anxiety was high, and my mind was all over the place. I was debating hard on whether I wanted to get out of the car or let her out and speed away. "Don't do it, bitch. Get out the car. Besides, I have a surprise for you." The smirk on her face made me nervous. What kind of surprise could she possibly have for me on the inside of a club?

"Don't be on no bullshit, Robin. I swear I'll leave your ass at this club," I warned her.

"Girl shut up and come on," she said once more. Hesitantly, I stepped out of the car.

Tossing my keys to the valet, we walked over to the bouncer. Robin whispered something in his ear, and he let us in without a problem. The people standing in the line started yelling out obscenities, but we kept walking like we didn't hear anything. I noticed that when we got to the door, Robin turned around and blew a kiss to them. I knew she was taunting them. All I could do was shake my head. If somebody would've thrown something and hit her in the top of her head, I would've just laughed because she knew she was wrong for messing with those folks.

"You gonna get enough of antagonizing people," I told her once we were inside the club and out of eye and earshot of the people outside.

"Girl, please. They can't be mad because we have pull. Now, come with me," she told me.

Making our way through the crowd, the tension in my body started to ease as the sound of the music started flowing through my body. The sight of the people dancing around and enjoying themselves was a great visual. I loved when our people could come together for a good time and there was no violence involved.

Robin's mouth was moving like she was trying to say something to me, but I couldn't hear her over the music. She didn't stop to try to make sure I could hear her either. She kept walking like she was on a mission. I did my best to keep up with her. We were headed to an area that was roped off. I figured that was the VIP section. What I didn't understand was why she was going over there. We hadn't paid for one and as far as I knew, we didn't know anybody who would've. That was until I looked up and saw Twist.

If Twist was there, that meant that Scorpio wasn't too far behind. Moving closer to Robin, I was anxious to see how things were going to play out.

"I'm glad you made her leave before I had to tear this whole club up about my man," she said as Twist pushed past Scorpio and pulled her in for an embrace.

That was something new to me. Robin didn't really cater to relationships. In fact, I can't remember the last time I saw her with a man in public because she was always with an older man or a man that belonged to someone else. Seeing her smile as she hugged Twist, out in this open area, was a shocker for me.

"What's up, ma?" he asked.

"Hey baby! I thought I'd take you up on that offer from earlier," she said and placed a kiss on his lips.

Scorpio and I locked eyes, but he didn't say anything to me. A few minutes into our stare off, he walked over to the chair closest to him and took a seat.

"Go get your man, girl," Robin told me and pushed me further into the section in Scorpio's direction.

It took me a minute, but I finally made my way a little closer to him.

"Hey," I dryly stated. He hit me with a head nod and kept vibin' to the music. "I'm sorry, I said hey," I repeated. He hit me with another head nod. That started to agitate me. "Didn't somebody ever teach you that you're supposed to speak when spoken to?"

"First of all, you're not my momma so you can get on with that. I spoke to you when I hit you with the head nod. Just because I didn't open my mouth didn't mean I didn't speak. What, nobody ever taught you about gestures?"

"Who you talking to like that?" I was offended. My hands flew up to my hips as I stood over him.

"Stop standing over me like that. It ain't cute, ma, and I don't fuck with bitches with bad attitudes," he informed me.

"Bitches?" Glancing around the VIP, I was checking to see if there were any other females in there besides Robin and me. Scorpio had me fucked up if he thought I was about to let him get away with talking crazy to me. "It's just a word. Stop trying to find a reason to argue with me," he returned.

As I was about to walk away, he hopped up from his seat. He grabbed my wrist and backed me up on the wall that was behind us.

"Don't ever walk away from me when I'm talking to you. You hear me? I'm not Javi and I don't do that dumb shit," he announced. The mention of Javi's name caused my skin to crawl. It also made me think about the things he'd done to me and what I didn't want to have to deal with again. Just that quick, I was ready to shut down and head home.

"Excuse me," I stated, trying to move around him.

"Didn't I just tell you about that walking away shit? We don't do that. We talk shit out and we don't do all that yelling and shit," he commented.

"Who is we? Where is this we stuff coming from? I'm not your woman," I fussed.

"Yeah, that's what your mouth says, but I can guarantee your body is telling you something completely different," he rebutted.

"I'm not about to do this with you. Move out of my way," I insisted. He looked at me as if I didn't say shit. That started to infuriate me. Robin was in her own little world talking to Twist, so she wasn't paying any attention to what was going on with me and Scorpio.

"I'm not moving. We both know that's not what you want. You can keep trying to fight me if you want to, but you know I'm right."

"You don't know me or what I want. Move like I asked you."

"Fine, I don't have to beg anybody. If I move then you don't have to worry about me coming at you again," he said. I smiled. That was a lie. Every time he saw me, he was going to be on me. We both knew that. So, being who I was, I tested the limit.

"Move!" I directed him for the final time. Scorpio threw his hands up in defeat and moved out of the way. It stunned me because I really felt he would've fought a little harder. I can't lie, it made me feel some type of way.

"You ready to talk to me now?" A chick I'd never seen before came waltzing into the VIP. She went straight over to Scorpio and asked to speak to him like I wasn't standing there.

Scorpio glimpsed at me before focusing his attention on the chick.

"Yeah," he said. My mouth dropped.

"Pick your mouth up, sweetie. I've watched you from the time you entered the club until the time you rejected him. You're a damn fool and I'm not. Don't get upset with me because I know how not to let a good thing go," she said in my ear.

Scorpio picked up his drink and went to say something to Twist. Robin came over to where me and the chick were and proceeded to stare her up and down.

"What's up?" she asked me.

"Nothing. Nothing at all," I replied.

"What? She came over here to take our drink order or something?" Robin kept her eyes on the unknown female.

"Drink order? Bitch, I don't work here." As soon as the word bitch came out of her mouth, my body tensed back up. Robin didn't have hoe in her blood and was not about to let this woman that we didn't know, slide after calling her out of her name.

"Could've fooled me. What other reason would you have to be over here if you aren't taking drink or food orders?"

"Don't worry about it. You'll see when I walk out of here with Scorpio on my arm."

"Boop... Bitch please!" Robin stated as she mushed the girl in the forehead. "I'm not my girl. I'll beat your ass and consider talking to you about it later. Right now, I'ma need for you to take your thirsty, trout mouth ass out of this section."

The girl stood there laughing like Robin hadn't said shit. Normally, I was the cool, calm, and collected one out of the two of us, but this chick was pushing my buttons. The fact that Scorpio was about to leave with her didn't make the situation better. He was fine, he was paid, and he appeared to want me for me and not for what I could give him. I'd be a fool to let the next chick have that. That much I knew. What was sad was that I had to see another woman going after him before I realized how stupid I'd been with him.

"Matter fact, you need to find you something safe to do because this ain't it," I chimed in. The stunned expression on Robin's face let me know that I'd done an excellent job with my comeback.

"Do we have a problem?" Scorpio and Twist came over to see what was going on.

"As of right now, there is no problem. This bitch ain't got shit on me. If you try to leave out of this section with her, I'm going to hit you so hard on the top of your head with that bottle that you're going to shit out your brain," I warned him.

"Damn bitch, you gutter," Robin exclaimed.

"Wow. You got a crazy bi-" Twist's words were cut off by the mean mug I shot him before he could get the whole word out. "I meant broad on your hand. You better leave her alone before she fucks you up," Twist informed Scorpio, chuckling.

"She not shakin' shit. She talkin' to hear herself talk. She'll be okay," he refuted and was about to walk past me.

Immediately, I grabbed his wrist and with all my might, pushed him against the same wall he had me pinned up against. He was about to say something, but I used my mouth to cover his. When his tongue slithered inside of my mouth, I felt like I was in heaven. Just to be a near a man was one thing. To be near this man was something different.

"What are you doing, Scorpio? You're supposed to be leaving with me," the woman announced.

"Shut up hoe, you see he busy," I heard Robin say. I attempted to pull away from Scorpio so I could address her, but he pulled me back in. Rubbing his hands over my ass, a soft moan escaped my mouth. His dick was rising and was poking me in the stomach. That caused me to jump back. I'd never experienced anything that big. It had me scared as hell.

"What you jumping for?" He smirked. All I could do was point at his dick. "He won't bite, unless you want him to." He chuckled. He displayed a grin so big; I probably could've counted all of his teeth.

"My nigga," Twist expressed, and the two men dapped each other up.

"We leaving or not, Labarron?" the woman asked, stomping her feet with her hands across her chest.

"Not hoe! Now bounce," I spoke through clenched teeth.

"You heard my girl," Scorpio chimed in, having my back. I was loving that shit already. The fact that he called me his girl made it ten times better. That was some shit Javi never would've done for me. He would've left me standing there with egg on my face.

The chick stormed out of the section. That only made me make a mental note to always watch my surroundings. Messing with Scorpio was going to come with baggage. That I was sure of. It meant I was going to have to wear tough skin at all times. That was something I wasn't sure I was ready for.

Chapter Fourteen:

Javi

Sitting back in the cut inside of one of my favorite clubs, I was chillin' before I had to go back home to Shawnte's naggin' ass. Had I known it was going to be like this when I got out, I would've stuck with Mignon. She at least knew how to shut the fuck up when a nigga told her to.

My head bobbed as I grooved to the music. I was enjoying my surroundings until I saw Mignon and her hoeish friend, Robin, come prancing inside. Mignon looked gorgeous as hell. I'd never seen her dress like that before. It made me miss her even more. When I was getting up to go talk to her, I noticed Robin guiding her towards the VIP section. Imagine my surprise when I saw them go in there with Twist and Scorpio. That nigga was really messing with my sloppy seconds. That was something I wasn't going to tolerate. He had to go.

My eyes stayed trained on them the whole time. A little bit of hope came to me when I saw her about to leave. That was until that bitch Aniya stepped in and fucked that up. She just had to go her duck faced ass over there fuckin' with Scorpio.

Mignon wasn't the type of chick that would start a fight, but she would finish it if she had to. If she wasn't going to mess with Scorpio before, she surely was about to do it now. That was my fault though. She was good to me and another woman still swooped in and stole me. You think she was about to let that happen again? Any woman who thought they were going to take a man from her at this point was sadly mistaken.

Aniya stormed out of the section and made her way towards the restroom. I was hot on her ass. As soon as she opened the door to enter, I placed my hand over her mouth and forced her the rest of the way inside. Checking the restroom, I made sure no one else was in there before locking the door.

"What the fuck are you doing?" she screamed once I removed my hand.

"What does it look like I'm doing? I'm trying to have a conversation with you," I said.

"Seems to me that you were trying to kidnap me and rape me or something. You know you don't have to do all that Javi. I've had my eyes on you for a while. I'd give it up with no problem," she said and licked her lips. She used one of her hands to run it down my chest. The further she went, the thirstier she seemed. I grabbed her hand right when she was about to wrap it around my dick.

"What the fuck? Don't tell me you're gay or something. I'm fine as fuck so there's no reason for you or any other man to turn me down," she fussed.

"If pussy is the only thing you have to offer, then that's plenty of reason for us to turn your ass down," I implied to her.

"Who said pussy was all I could offer? You clearly don't know me," she retorted.

"I'm not here for all that. I need to talk business."

"What kind of business?" She folded her arms across her chest and frowned up at me. She was disappointed that I wasn't trying to slide off in her. Don't get me wrong, she was sexy as hell. Sex just wasn't on my mind right then.

"We both share a common interest. You want Scorpio, for whatever reason and I want Mignon."

"For whatever reason." She rolled her eyes.

"We not bout to do this, Aniya. Either we gonna work together to get what we want, or you can move around."

"You came to me for help. I'm pretty sure I got this."

"Naw, you don't. Mignon's a good girl. Once Scorpio sees just how good she is, you won't stand a chance at getting him back."

"If she was so good, then why aren't you with her?"

"I was stupid as hell. I've learned my lesson and now that I'm trying to get back with her, neither of them are making it easy for me. You wanna help me end this shit before it starts or you gonna keep trying your luck alone? Two heads are better than one." I don't know why I felt compelled to reason with her. It seemed to me that she wasn't really interested in getting with Scorpio. Something else was up with her.

"I got me. You worry about you." She acted as if she was about to walk away. Suddenly, she came back to me and dropped down to her knees. Unbuckling my belt, I watched as she pulled my semi-erect dick out of my pants and insert it into her mouth. My head fell back as I enjoyed the pleasure she was giving me. It had been so long since I had some good ass head that I almost nutted up within the first few minutes. A nigga wasn't ready to bust yet.

Picking her up, lifting her dress up, I snatched her thong off and sat her on the counter. Trying to enter her was hard as hell because she was dryer than frozen bread. I had to spit on my hand three times and rub it between her legs before she was wet enough for me to enter. Scorpio had to have loved her to stay with her as long as he did. Ain't no bitch worth walking around with carpet burn on my dick.

It took me trying to slide in and out of her a few times for me to know she wasn't what I wanted. I couldn't stay hard and she couldn't stay wet. That shit felt like I had splinters on my dick.

"I'm good, ma. I gotta get home to my girl," I lied. I grabbed some paper towels and put some soap on it before proceeding to clean my dick off. I had more than enough sense to know that if I went home smelling like another bitch, Shawnte was going to have a fit. She was already going to go off because I left her and went out. I didn't need any extra shit for her to fuss about.

"Girl? What damn girl? Why you in here trying to conspire with me to get with that fat bi-" No sooner than she was about to finish her statement, my hands were wrapped around her throat. She had me fucked up. I did Mignon bad true enough, but nobody else was going to get the chance to.

"You put some muthafuckin' RESPECT on her name! You hear me?" She couldn't speak so she just nodded her head in understanding.

Bam... Bam... Bam...

Beating on the door was her saving grace. I dropped her and was prepared to leave until she said something smart.

"Fuck you and your bitch!" I kicked her dead in her face, and she slumped over. I picked her up and sat her down on one of the bathroom stalls. Locking the stall, I crawled under it so I could get out of the restroom.

Bam... Bam... Bam...

The beating came again. Checking myself, I made sure my clothes were good. I got her thong off the floor and tossed it in the trash before finally unlocking the door.

"You do see that this is the women's restroom, right?" some bald mouth woman said to me.

"You do see my dick hard and my girl is in a stall over there sleep with her thumb in her mouth cuz I beat those guts in, right? Find you some fuckin' business, Karen!"

Strolling past her, I exited the club before someone really figured out what was up with Aniya. There was no reason for me to go to jail behind someone that had a trashy pussy and didn't belong to me. Besides, Scorpio and Mignon were nowhere to be found so there was really no reason for me to remain there. The wheels in my head were turning as I prepared myself to head home to Shawnte. As if the night wasn't already long, I knew it was going to be even longer once I was face to face with her.

Chapter Fifteen:

Mignon

(Two Weeks Later...)

Waking up smiling was something I hadn't done in a while. That was all because of Scorpio. He was much more different of a guy than I thought he would be. However, I still kept him at a distance because I refused to be hurt again. The shit with Javi really did something to me.

Ring... Ring... Ring...

I was coming out of the bathroom to grab something when my phone started ringing. Apparently, I wasn't moving fast enough because it stopped ringing before I could reach it. Still needing to handle my hygiene so I could get ready for work, I rushed back inside of the bathroom. The minute I turned the water on to brush my teeth, the phone started ringing again.

Ring... Ring... Ring...

"Hell- FUCKKKKKK!" I screamed as I stubbed my pinky toe on the nightstand near my bed when I was trying to grab my phone from under my pillow.

"What kind of greeting is that?" The sound of his voice had me wanting to melt. My pussy was throbbing. My panties were sopping wet. We hadn't even had sex yet and he already had some type of hold on my pussy. That wasn't something he was going to hear from me anytime soon though. There was no way his head needed to be any bigger than it already was.

"Hey big head! What are you doing?" I replied, trying to play off the excitement I had just from hearing his voice.

"How you know my head big?"

"It's not like you don't make it a point for me to see you every day."

"Oh, you talking about that head?" he joked.

"Shut up, silly." There I was, giggling like a schoolgirl. That was not like me at all. I'm not sure what he was doing to me, but I was loving every minute of it.

"What you bout to do, baby?"

"I'm getting ready to go to work. What about you?"

"Work? What I tell you about all that work stuff? I told you that as long as we are together, I got you," he reminded me. He's told me that ever since we made shit with us official. However, I was still scared to give him that much trust. If he really wanted me to walk away from my job, it was going to take more than two weeks worth of conversation and promises that could be broken at any time.

"We are not about to have this conversation again. Now what are you about to get into?" I asked again.

"You know I'm just trying to get you to focus on school so you can be done with it. You've been doing all that working and not seeing any benefits from it. Live for yourself sometimes." He'd often told me that. I understood what he meant, but it was hard from me to walk away from what I'd been doing. No, I didn't have to take care of Javi anymore. That didn't change the fact that for the past two and a half years, I'd developed a routine and it was hard to break it.

"I am living for myself. I'm talking to you, aren't I?" I giggled at the thought of me being with someone that was the complete opposite of me. Javi and I had a few similarities, but if you asked me, Scorpio and I barely had anything in common.

"You need to let me talk to that pussy. It's been two weeks. How long do you expect a nigga like me to wait?" he questioned.

"I'm not read yet," I admitted. It wasn't that I didn't like Scorpio, because I really did. It was me not wanting to rush anything. The one thing I didn't want was for our relationship to be built on sex and not love and trust. Not to mention, the fact that I wasn't what he normally dated still bothered me. That was something I wasn't prepared to tell him yet.

"When will you be ready?"

"I honestly don't know. It's not now. If you can't take that then you need to talk to someone else," I snapped. I removed the phone from my ear at that point because the line went dead silent. Knowing what had happened, I put the phone down on my nightstand and continued to get ready for work.

It bothered me that Scorpio had hung upon me, but I knew it was my fault because he didn't deserve me snapping on him the way that I did. If anything, I could've said what I said in a better manner. He had to understand that I was still upset about being hurt and was only doing what I could to prevent it from happening again. Why was that so hard for him to catch on to?

Chapter Sixteen:

Scorpio

"Aye, what's up?"

"Hey baby! I was expecting your call. How are you?"

"A nigga horny as fuck. Pull up!"

"I'll be there in ten minutes, baby."

It was fucked up that I had to call on another woman to please me because mine didn't want to get on her job. I'm not saying it's a must that a nigga beat that back in during the first night or two, but we'd been rockin' for two weeks. Mignon needed to step up and handle business. If not, shit like this was prone to happen.

Knowing that I needed to take a shower, I made a call to India. She had been my housekeeper for years. She needed to know that I was having company. All I wanted her to do was to answer the door when Aniya's thirsty ass arrived. Aniya knew her way around the crib because we used to be hot and heavy at one point. She'd find her way to the bedroom once India let her in.

Rolling to the edge of the bed, I set up and ran my hand down my face. My mind was on Mignon. It bothered me that I was about to fuck someone else. It also bothered me that she hadn't started to trust being with me yet. Waiting for her had been something I'd been doing since the first day I laid eyes on her years ago. There were plenty of times that I could've caught her in a vulnerable state and took advantage of her, but I didn't. There was no need for me to do all of that because I truly believed that when the time was right, we'd both know it.

Inside the courthouse that day, it seemed like God had spoken to me and told me to make my move. Yeah, I sin all the time. That doesn't take away the fact that I have a heavy belief in God. I have to pray constantly. Especially, with the line of work that I was in.

Finally standing up, I entered my master bathroom and turned the shower on. Not bothering to wait for it to warm up, I stepped in and allowed the cold water to beat off my body. That was something I always did, it helped me wake up faster.

"Fuck!" I stated as soon as the cold water hit me. Thank God I had gas. That made my water heat up quicker and it got hotter than normal.

Ring... Ring... Ring...

My phone rung and I immediately knew who it was. I could tell by the ringtone that it was Mignon calling back. She must've finished getting ready for work and was ready to talk to me. It was cool. She was going to have to learn that I was in charge in this relationship and she was not about to handle me anyway that she wanted.

Staying in the shower for ten minutes, I made sure I was clean from top to bottom before stepping out and drying off. I wrapped a towel around my waist and strolled inside my bedroom. There she was. Naked as the day she was born. The sun shining in through the blinds was causing her body to glow. She had her legs spread wide open as she played with her pretty pink, freshly shaved pussy.

"Hey baby! I knew it would be a matter of time before you called me," she announced. "Come talk to this pearl, baby."

"Naw. I didn't call you over here to make love and shit. I need you to suck this dick, let me fuck you in the ass and you can bounce," I bluntly spoke.

"Damn. Why you talking to me like that? You've never been that way with me before?"

"I didn't know you were a hoe before. You showed me otherwise. Now, either we are going to do this my way or not at all."

Aniya rolled her eyes. It didn't take her long to think about what she was about to fuck up if she didn't do what I said. She wasn't going to risk getting this good dick, so she abruptly got on her knees and crawled to the edge of the bed where I was standing, stroking my semi-erect dick.

Aniya grabbed ahold of my dick and began stroking it herself. I relaxed my body so I could enjoy what she was about to do to me. There was no way I could front. Aniya had the mouth of an anaconda; she could suck anything down. Her head game was on point and that was something neither of us could deny. The moment she clamped her mouth around my dick, I threw my head back to enjoy it. She was slurping and sucking on it like she was sucking on a turkey neck.

"Fuck ma!" I exclaimed. It was feeling so good.

Ring... Ring... Ring...

The phone rang again. It was Mignon calling back. That fucked with my mental. It made me feel worse about what I was doing? She was calling to probably try to make shit right and there I was ignoring her and getting my dick sucked. The thought caused me to feel sick to my stomach. There was no way I could do that to her. Immediately, I pulled back from Aniya.

"What's wrong, baby? Did I scrap you with my teeth or something?"

"Naw. I can't do this. I need you to leave," I told her.

"What? Leave for what? You called me."

"I know that. I was wrong. You got to bounce, ma."

"No. I'm not bouncing until I get some dick," she hollered.

"That's fine by me."

Going into my closet, I went into the box Aniya left when I put her ass out. Picking it up, I walked it right over to her. Once I handed it to her, I pointed to the door to let her know that I still wanted her to take her trifling ass on.

"This some bullshit," she said once she opened the box. "What the fuck am I going to do with this?"

"The same thing you was doing with it when I was gone or when you were with other niggas," I chided. "Now, get the fuck on," I told her once more.

Inside the box were a bunch of lil sex toys I found. She had that shit hidden in a shoe box in the closet and when I had her shit removed, it was left. It tripped me out that she never called to try to get the shit.

"This shit is old. I had this before you and I even got together."

"Then why was it in my house?"

"I've had it forever and I've never gotten rid of it. When I started moving my shit in, it was just one of the things I grabbed. You know I never had to use any of it because you always handled business," she called herself explaining.

"You don't have to tell me that. I know the power of my dick."

"Did you forget the power of my pussy?"

"Naw. I ain't forget shit about your pussy. Why you think I told you to suck my dick and let me fuck you in the ass?" I couldn't help but laugh. Her pussy was garbage as fuck. It was my love for her that kept me with her. Damn shame, huh?

"What is that supposed to mean?"

"If you don't know, then neither do I." The expression on her face was one of confusion. What she was confused about beat the hell out of me.

"No. You big and bad, say what you gotta say, Labarron."

"First, stop calling me by my muthafuckin' government. We not the same couple we used to be. That means you lost that fuckin' privilege."

"I know you not dissing me because of that fat bitch. She's not even your type."

"Don't disrespect her like that."

"Clearly you're the one disrespecting her. You talking to her blimp body ass, but you got me in your bedroom. What? She not giving you known of that stale pussy yet?"

"Have you ate her pussy or fucked her? How the fuck would you know? Furthermore, quit calling her fat. Is she a size 0, hell no. That means she knows that she's beautiful and loves the skin that she's in. That's the only type of woman I want. I woman that's confident in herself and don't have to put the next woman down just to make herself feel good. Why the fuck am I even explaining this to a bitch who can't even get her pussy wet? You need to go to the doctor and get that shit checked out. Right after you get your shit and get the fuck out of here." Just that quick, she'd angered.

That was one thing I honestly couldn't stand, a woman putting down another woman. Especially, when they were black women. Those be the first ones hollering, "Support black businesses," or "Black girl magic," and don't mean shit behind it.

"Fuck you, Scorpio. You act like everything about you is perfect. It's not. A lot of those orgasms were faked anyways," she yelled. I laughed so hard that I had to grab ahold of my stomach. That bitch was cappin' her ass off. I knew my dick was good and so did the many bitches that was blessed to feel it. If it was as bad as she was claiming it was, then I could guarantee none of those women would still be calling me trying to get me to fuck them.

Aniya talked shit the whole time she was putting her clothes back on. Nothing that she said or did moved me. She was wrong and she knew it. She was mad about the fact that she'd fucked up and lost out on her good thing. All she had to do was be loyal to me and she would've had the world. Shit, I thought I was giving her the world. Then the only excuse she could've gave me for stepping out was that she didn't like that I was in the streets more than I was with her. That shouldn't have been a problem because she knew what it was when she got with me. She knew I was busy trying to build an empire.

"Is everything okay, sir?" India entered the room and asked. I'm sure that was due to all of the screaming Aniya's ass was doing.

"Yeah. I'm straight. Aniya was about to leave. Please make sure she does," I directed and walked inside the bathroom. Turning the shower back on, I was getting ready to get inside.

Ring... Ring... Ring...

Mignon was calling back again. I heard the phone when it started ringing then it suddenly stopped. I didn't think anything about it. In my mind, I figured she'd gotten tired of it ringing and going to voicemail, so she ended the call before she got the voicemail again. That was until I heard hollering.

"Yeah bitch. You thought you had my nigga, but you see who he here with."

"What the fuck are you doing?" I snarled as soon as I stepped back inside the bedroom and saw Aniya on my phone. She knew damn well that I didn't go for that shit. Even when we were together, I told her that I'd break her damn fingers if she was caught with my phone.

"Ain't shit changed. Now I'm going to have to fuck you up," I fumed, snatching the phone from her.

"Mignon? Baby, it's not what you think," I tried to explain.

"Save it! You're no better than Javi's ass," she cried and hung up without giving me the chance to explain.

Aniya stood before me with a silly smile on her face. I wasn't the type of man that hit women, but fuck that.

Smack...

Aniya at that point was no longer a woman. She was a dead bitch!

"Why'd you hit me? You promised you'd never hit me? Do you love her and not me anymore?"

"Love ain't got shit to do with this. You fucked up when you touched my fuckin' phone. Then you knew it was her and you did that shit to patronize her. That was fucked up and you know it!" I grunted.

Aniya had me fucked all the way up. The bitch had lost her shit. Did I regret hitting her? I probably should have, but I didn't. She had that shit coming. I bet her ass won't touch my damn phone again.

Chapter Seventeen:

Javi

"Right there, baby. Right there! Fuck your pussy. Damn, you feel so good," Shawnte moaned as I fucked her from behind. We'd been arguing for the past two days and I was over it. The only way I was able to get her to shut up was to dick her down good, which was what I was doing.

Shawnte threw her ass back and in a circle as I pounded in and out of her. I allowed her to fuck me as I stayed still and watched my dick glide in and out of her.

"Fuck ma. That shit feels so good!" I exclaimed as I enjoyed the pleasure I was receiving. Out of nowhere, thoughts of Mignon entered my mind. Fuckin' her was so much better than fuckin' Shawnte. Mignon's pussy was wetter, tighter, and fatter. Then she had her little love handles that I really enjoyed grabbing on to while I hit her from the back. Doggy style was my favorite position and she knew that. She knew my body so well that whenever I started to tire out in one position or wasn't moaning as much, she automatically knew to switch that shit up. With Shawnte, I had to direct her every move. It had gotten old.

Maybe I was looking for a reason to complain so I could leave. Although, I didn't know where I'd be able to go. Mignon was really done with me and by the looks of things, she was letting shit with Scorpio get heavy. Never in a million years would I have thought that she wouldn't keep taking my shit or that she would end up with the nigga that employed me. I constantly looked for ways to break them up. If I was able to get Aniya to work with me that night, I'm sure they would've been over and done with by now.

"You okay, baby? You wanna try another position?" Shawnte asked me, removing me from my thoughts. Instead of responding to her, I fiercely pushed in and out of her until I was ready to bust.

"Fuck baby! Get on your knees. Here it comes," I instructed her. She turned and frowned up instead of doing what I said so I nutted all in her face.

"Aaaghhhhh... I can't believe you did that shit," she cried before running to the bathroom. I laid down on the bed and went back to my thoughts of Mignon. That's when I decided it was time to try a different approach with her. Picking my phone up from under the pillow, I decided to send her a text. She didn't have my number so it would be easier for me to get her to talk to me. At least, I thought it would.

Me: Hey Mignon! HRU? Hit me back ASAP Rocky!

Ten minutes passed and I got no response. That started to bother me. It was a new number so there was no reason she would know it was me. She was nosey as hell so she wasn't the type of person that would not answer a call because she didn't know who it was. It started to annoy me. I decided to send her another text to see what the problem was.

Me: I no u got my text. Wat's up, ma? U good?

After a few minutes, my phone finally notified me of an incoming text. I smiled. The only person it could've been was Mignon. I contemplated in my head what I could respond to her if she only said hi or if she asked who I was. My smile grew bigger when I finally read the message.

Mignon: Stop texting me. I know it's you, Scorpio. I don't want anything to do with you now or ever. I'm not these other women that you can get over on. I don't need you or your money. Now, leave me alone before I get a restraining order against you.

There was trouble in paradise which was right up my alley. That meant I had a chance to get back with her. If I played my cards right, she'd be mine again in no time. I couldn't wait to get the hell away from Shawnte's salty ass.

Me: Cum again? Dis ain't no damn Scorpio. Dat nigga cud neva b me. Dis Javi. I fuk'd up. Plz meet up wit me so I can x'plain.

Mignon: I should've known by the fucked-up grammar that it was you. No, I don't want to meet up with you and no, I don't want your ass back. Stay over there with you Pitbull. You fucked up and now you have to live with it.

My eyes damn near bulged out of my head when I read her message. She had a lot of damn nerve thinking it was okay for her to talk to me sideways like that. That was shit she knew I didn't tolerate. I'm sure the only reason she was doing it was because we were no longer together. That didn't mean a damn thing to me. She still had to respect me.

"The shower's running, baby. Come on before the water gets cold," Shawnte announced as she came trampling back into the room. Her plastic ass swayed from side to side as she came towards me. She was trying to get close enough to see what I was doing on the phone, so I made it a point to close the screen out before she saw anything. She pouted, but she never said anything about it. She knew better. I'm sure the bitch tried to go through my phone when I was sleep. That couldn't happen because I was slick with my shit. I always made sure I wiped the phone clean whenever I was done talking and texting. Then, I had a hidden folder that she couldn't find unless she went through certain apps to get to it. She never had my phone in her possession long enough for that to happen, so I wasn't worried one bit.

"Here I come. I'm checkin' with somebody about a job. Have you thought about getting one?"

"What? Who? I know damn well you didn't ask me about no damn job again. You told me you were going to take care of me when you hit these streets. Did you forget that we have a child to take care of?"

"Yeah, I forgot. Shit the author of this book probably forgot too because the baby ain't ever here and she ain't said shit else about him."

"All I'm saying is that you told me that you were going to make sure I was straight. You did that up until the time you got out of jail. Maybe you need to go back to that bitch and keep sending me money. This shit right here not working," she nagged.

"You're right, it's not. It's time for me to move on. So, let me go ahead and tell you that I do want to go back to Mignon. If I can get her to forgive me, then that's exactly where I'll be heading. So, you might as while be looking for another nigga to hold you down cuz that ain't me. Women hold me down, I don't hold their asses down," I advised her. I meant that shit. Fuck I'ma take care of someone for when someone could be taking care of me?

Chapter Eighteen:

Shawnte

Javi had me fucked up. I rode with him all those years and he came out telling me nothing but lies. He made so many promises to me while he was locked up and I believed every one of them. My mother constantly told me to stay away from niggas like him. Did I listen? Clearly not. I was paying for it now. He wasn't the man I thought he was going to be. I swear it was so much better when he was locked up and selling me a pipe dream. At least then, I was able to move the way that I wanted to.

"Get out, Javi," I hollered at him as soon as he mentioned going back to Mignon. Did he think that shit was going to bother me? It didn't. Hell, if he did go, I wouldn't have to deal with a crybaby ass nigga, which was clearly what he was.

"Get out? Girl bye! I'm not going anywhere. Not until I get ready to go. You can do us both a favor and stay out of my way," he ordered before storming out of the room. Evidently, he didn't know who he was fuckin' with. I wasn't Mignon. I'd torture the fuck out of his ass and send him home to his mother, unidentifiable.

"Fine. Stay around. I bet you won't be staying too long. I'm going to make shit as uncomfortable as possible for you."

"Try it and see won't your mother have to go down to the morgue to identify your body," he threatened me. The look in his eye had me shook. I'd never seen it before and surely didn't want to see it again. That's why I hurried and snapped my damn mouth shut.

Two hours later and Javi was on his way out the door. Where he was going? I didn't know. I knew not to ask him where he was going either. However, I was going on a little trip of my own. See, I'd been following Mignon for the longest. I knew her schedule and routine like I knew the back of my hand. Since Javi wanted to play games with me, I was going to pay Mignon a little visit. If she ended up getting fired in the process, that was her business. She was not about to have an easy time trying to take my man away from me.

It wasn't long after Javi left on his bike that I took off in my car. If I was right, Mignon was at her check cashing job. She worked the front counter, so she'd have no choice other than to tend to my needs. As I arrived at her job, I checked myself in the mirror to make sure my makeup and hair was on point. There was no way I was going in front of my man's ex and without letting her see me at my best. She needed to look at me and see exactly what it was about me that made him leave her ass.

"Welcome to Speedy Cash," she yelled out as I entered. Not once did she look up at me. She was busy helping the person at the counter. I patiently waited until she was done before I walked up to her.

"Hello. I'd like to do a cash advance," I told her. When she finally looked up, you would've thought she'd seen a ghost by the expression on her face. "You good?" I asked, knowing damn well I didn't care. On the inside, I was filled with joy that I was able to get to her the way that I was.

"Yeah, I'm great. How may I assist you?" she asked, keeping things professional so far. That meant I wasn't doing what I set out to do. I needed to push her buttons and get her riled up. That way, I could file a complaint against her so she could lose her job.

"I already told you that I needed a cash advance," I shouted.

"Please lower your voice, ma'am. Now, are you asking for a cash advance or check advance?" she asked.

"Bitch don't try to be funny with me. You know what I came in here for."

Instead of responding to me, she walked away from the counter. She didn't say, "go to hell", "kiss my ass", "suck my big toe", or nothing. All she did was walk away. I watched as she was in the back of the store speaking with whom I assumed was the supervisor. They both returned to talk to me together.

"Sir, we are going to need you to lower your voice. This is a place of business and we need you to treat it as such," the woman told me.

"Sir? Who the fuck are you referring to as sir?" I asked. Mignon was in tears laughing and yet, I didn't find anything to be funny.

"My bad." We engaged in an intense stare down in front of Mignon, who didn't say a word.

"How can we help you?"

"You can help me by telling me who the manager is."

"I am the manager. My name is Shelby. How can we help you?" she asked again.

"Well, Shelby, I was trying to explain to your little worker here," I said, being sure to point my finger at Mignon, "that I needed to take out a cash advance. Her attitude was so bad that she couldn't even assist me with my request."

"I'm sorry that she handled you so poorly. I'll be more than happy to assist you. Can you please hand me your debit card or a check?" she insisted.

"Hand you that for what? I don't have money in my account," I barked. "If I did, I wouldn't be coming in here for an advance," I added.

"That's why you and Javi are perfect for each other; you're both broke," Mignon commented.

"What you say, bitch? I got money."

"Yet you just said that you didn't. What are you really doing in here? If you came in here to start trouble, then you might as well be on the opposite side of the door because I'm not about to let you cost me my job. You know what that is, right? A place normal people go to on a daily basis to make the money they need for their bills.

I'm sure you wouldn't know anything about that though," she remarked.

"Fuck you mean? I have money and can afford my damn bills, hoe. You gave me the money, remember?" I threw a cheap shot at her. The smile that was once on her face quickly vanished.

"Not in here, Mignon. Let's get her done so she can leave," Shelby told her.

"Why you rushing me to leave? I must've taken your man too. You can call me the man snatcher," I joked. Neither of them laughed, but I sure as hell did.

"Yeah. Keep thinking messing with other people men is a good thing. One day you're going to catch something you can't get rid of," she muttered.

"Oh, like I caught your man and can't get rid of him? You right, suh!" She suddenly started laughing. "What the fuck is so funny?" I asked.

"Shelby, I know she's not talking about this man right here. The one that keeps texting and calling me, begging me to take him back." Shelby's eyes got big. She didn't know what to say so she remained quiet.

Javi told me he was going to try to get back with her. He didn't say he was already doing the shit. It had me wondering what else he had been doing behind my back. I was pissed. She wasn't going to see that though. I came in here to get her fired and I wasn't going to leave until I did just that.

"Mignon, you need to go to the back if you can't remain professional," Shelby finally opened her cock sucker to speak.

"She's very unprofessional and I will be reporting that to corporate," I informed them both.

"That's fine. You have every right to do so. However, I need for you to tell me how I can assist you so that I can help the next person in line."

"Don't be rushing me, bitch."

"You are really working my patience right now. I'm trying to help you but you're making it very hard. If you came in here to start something with Mignon, then you need to leave. If you came in here because you really need money, then tell me what it is that you want so that I may assist you. If you keep being rude and disrespectful, I will have to ask you to leave."

"You can't make me leave."

"I can and I will. I have the right to refuse service to anybody, ma'am. So, again, I ask you, how can I assist you?" she snarled.

"I'm trying to get some money. I don't have no check or none of that shit. I'm not trying to take it out of my account. I need for you to give me some money on a loan or some shit," I advised her.

"Oh, so you meant you needed a check advance?" she replied.

"What's the difference?" I queried.

"The difference is a cash advance is you drawing money off a card or an account that you already have. A check advance is us giving you a loan until payday. Is that what you're interested in?"

"No. Both of ya'll bitches is slow. Matter of fact, I'm interested in you firing her because she didn't do a good job. How can I call and report her as a worker?"

"Here's a sheet of paper. Write down everything you want me to know and I'll handle things accordingly." I could already tell that she was lying.

"Fine. I'll take my business somewhere else." I snatched my purse off the counter and left. Did I go there to accomplish what I wanted to? No. That was fine. Mignon just better know that she hadn't seen or heard the last of me.

Chapter Nineteen:

Mignon

(A Month Later...)

After hearing Aniya on Scorpio's phone, my mind was all over the place. He told me that he was going to do right by me, but he ended up being no better than Javi. I was glad I found out how he was before I decided to give myself to him.

Today, I had a lunch date. I was a little happy about it because it had been a long time coming. Since I had to be at work right after I ate, I decided to just wear my uniform. It consisted of some khaki pants and a green polo shirt. I threw on my Vans and put my hair up in a messy bun. Once I'd stuck my diamond studs in my ear, I was on my way out the door.

Robin tried to stop me to have a conversation, but I blew her off. It was wrong of me to do her that way. Yeah, I knew that. I just wasn't in the mood to be talking about Scorpio. That's all she wanted to talk about lately. I'm sure that had a lot to do with her making shit official with Twist. I was happy for my girl, but I wasn't in the business of being hurt again. I'd spend the rest of my life by myself before I allow another man to hurt me and make me damaged goods.

It didn't take me long to pull up in front of the restaurant. Finding a parking spot, I hoped out and made my way inside. My date was already sitting and waiting for me. As I approached the table, I noticed him standing to pull out my chair for me. That was a first for him.

"Thanks," I told him as he kissed my cheek. I was about to say something to him, but I didn't. If I did, then the date probably would've gone left real fast and I didn't feel like causing a scene.

"You look beautiful," he told me, causing me to blush.

"You don't have to lie to me. I know I look a mess. I had no choice but to wear my uniform since I have to get to work right after we leave here," I explained.

"You don't have to explain that to me. You know I've always loved you when you were in your natural state," he replied.

"Thanks, Javi. You can stop with the compliments now. What is this all about?" I questioned him. He kept begging me to meet up with him so he could explain what happened. At first, I told him no. There was really nothing for us to discuss. However, after speaking with my mother about the situation, it made more sense to have the conversation and get it over with. At least then, I won't have to worry about him consistently nagging me to meet him.

"What's wrong with me complimenting my girl?"

"Your girl? Let me go ahead and stop you right there. I'm not your girl. The only reason I even met up with you today was because I wanted you to stop reaching out to me. I can assure you that no matter what you tell me today, it's not going to change the fact that you hurt me when you didn't have to. If you weren't happy, then you should've said that."

"It wasn't that I wasn't happy. I was just confused on what I wanted."

"Confused? Nigga, what was there to be confused about? You had a woman out her busting her ass thinking she was saving money to get you one of the best attorney's that money could buy. I worked like a fuckin' slave at multiple jobs. You got my tax refunds, school refunds, and any money I had left from bills. Instead of using it for what it was for, you were financing the next bitch. Oh, you were happy. Happy screwing me over," I fussed.

"I told you that I fucked up. All I want to do is make it right. Come on, baby. Forgive me!" he pleaded with me.

"There's nothing to forgive. However, if it makes you feel better hearing me say those words, then I forgive you," I told him. Just because I said it didn't mean that I meant it. That nigga burned me to my soul and now he needed me. There was no going back for me. One thing about me, when I was done with your ass, I meant that shit.

It was a different story when it came to Scorpio. We never even had a fair chance at being together. I was pissed at Aniya answering the phone, yet I still cared about him. When he told me some of what happened, I believed him. Even though I didn't allow him to go into full detail of what went down. The only reason I was still acting upset with him was because I didn't think she should've been there in the first place. It had me thinking that every time we got into it, he was going to think it was okay for him to be with another chick and that shit wasn't cute nor was it something that I was willing to deal with. There will never be a chance for another bitch to be in an equation with my and my nigga again.

"Stop acting like you don't miss me."

"There was a time when I missed the hell out of you. I'm over that now. You took my money. Money that I struggled to come up with. You lied to me constantly. You had me looking like a damn fool. All you had to do was tell me you didn't see a future with us, and I could've gone on about my business. Instead, you acted like a little boy and not the man that you were supposed to be. I'm over that now."

"I allowed everything that was going on with me cloud my judgement. I swear I know I fucked up. I'm owning up to that. Doesn't that matter at all?"

"Maybe if you would've come to me right after it happened, it would've meant something to me. There's nothing you can say to me today or any other day to take away the pain that you've caused me. So, today, I'm asking that you stay away from me. When you chose that hoe over me, that was the last conversation we ever really should've had," I told him.

"I said I was sorry. Let me make this shit right."

"The only thing you can do to make it right at this point is to give me back what you took from me. I want every single dime that I sent to your ass back. I worked my ass off to come up with that money and I want it the fuck back. Until then, we have nothing to discuss."

"So, you're telling me that if I can come up with every penny that you sent me, then I have a chance of getting you to forgive me? Will we be able to work on our relationship then?" he questioned me.

"What I'm saying is that I want my money back. I've already forgiven you for what you did to me because I'll never give you that much power over me," I advised him.

"Power over you? What is that supposed to mean?" he quizzed.

"My mother always told me that when I allowed something someone else did bother me to the point that it disrupts my life, then I'm giving them power over me," I explained. "There is nothing you can say or do to have any control over my feelings or my life. I forgive you, but I'll never forget what you did. That in itself should be enough for you to know that there will never be another Javi and

Mignon again. Unless, you find another bitch with my name. You might as well stop trying," I confessed.

"I'm not letting you go," he snarled, reaching for my wrist.

"You got three seconds to get your dick beaters off my bitch or we're going to tear this muthafuckin' building up."

Scorpio's voice startled me. I never saw him enter the building. It made me wonder when he'd gotten there and how much he'd heard of the conversation.

"Your bitch? Nigga she is and always will be my bitch. Besides, she already told me that she wasn't fuckin' with you on that level," Javi spat.

All I could do was drop my head. I was super embarrassed at the way the shit was going down. How could I allow him to disturb my peace the way that he was doing? Something told me to stick to my first mind and avoid him at all cost. The ball was in my court with Scorpio. Now that he's seen me with Javi, there was no telling what the outcome was going to be. How could I be so damn stupid? I didn't even get a chance to confront Javi about his bitch popping up at my job. When was enough going to be enough?

Chapter Twenty:

Scorpio

Mignon still wasn't fuckin' with a nigga and she had every right not to. At the same time, I wasn't letting her ass go that easy. She could ignore my calls and text all she wanted. It was only going to be a matter of time before I had her ass back fuckin' with me. This time, we were going to move at my pace and not hers.

Javi was making stupid moves. He'd pissed Shawnte off and she was determined not to be without a man. She hit the streets trying to find me and when she did, she was quick to tell me about Javi's little thought of wanting to get back with Mignon. Obviously, I hoped that she would be smart enough not to go back to him. My hope wasn't enough. If she really wanted to be with him, she was going to do it. That's why I made it a point to keep tabs on their ass.

Shawnte told me that one day she pretended to be sleep and was able to get Javi's password. She sent me screenshots of conversations between Javi and Mignon. That allowed me to see everything they discussed, including the messages where she told him to kick rocks and the one where she agreed to meet up with him to hear him out. Not gonna lie, that shit had me a little worried. As long as she was keeping her distance from him, I left her alone. Shit changed when she decided she was going to let him get close to her. I didn't trust him as far as I could throw him so there was no way I was going to allow him to get near her without me being present to protect her.

When I found out where they were supposed to be meeting up at, I went to the restaurant and paid the owner to put me in a table where my back would be against theirs, but I would be close enough to hear their entire conversation.

Everything was cool until she started telling him that she didn't want to deal with him. It was like he was trying to force himself back into her life. When he told her that he wasn't going to let her go and I saw him grab ahold of a wrist, that was it for me. Either that nigga was going to let her go or he was going to be walking out of this bitch without his hands.

"You got three seconds to get your dick beaters off my bitch or we're going to tear this muthafuckin' building up,"

I warned him. It was more of a guaranteed promise. However, it was up to him how he chose to take it.

"Your bitch? Nigga she is and always will be my bitch. Besides, she already told me that she wasn't fuckin' with you on that level," he spat. The nigga had the audacity to smirk. I pulled my fist back and was about to punch him.

"Scorpio, NO!" I stopped as soon as I heard Mignon scream. She hated being caught up in mess and if I hit Javi, that was exactly what was going to happen. It was going to cause a very messy scene. I couldn't do that to her, so I rethought my decision and chose not to hit him. Please understand that it was a tough decision to make. Next time, his ass was not going to be so lucky. Jesus Christ himself could come down and tell me not to fuck that nigga up and he was still going to end up catching this fade.

"Why you protecting this nigga?" I quipped. Even though I knew what she was doing, I had to act like I was upset. That was my way of getting her to soften up a bit with me and leave with me. She'd previously been avoiding me, and this was the perfect opportunity to put an end to it and that's what I was planning on doing.

"I'm not protecting him. I don't want to cause a scene and I don't want you to end up in jail behind somebody who's not worth it. Please just stop it. Let's go somewhere and talk," she pleaded with me.

Even though I was going to go with her, I had to play the shit cool.

"You can't be serious. We came here to talk about us. How are you going to leave with this slime ball as nigga? He's never going to be me and you're never going to love him the way that you loved me. He sure as hell can't love you the way that I can," Javi tried to reason with her.

"Love me the way that you can? Love him the way I loved you? Let me tell you this, Javi. Your ass can cancel all that bullshit that you spitting to me. I don't want anybody to love me the way that you did. I deserve way more than that shit. Then you talking about going back to you. I'd never be able to be with you because every time you touched me; all I'd be able to think about was if you touched that bitch the way that you were touching me. We'd never work. I'm asking you for one last time to leave me alone. Don't reach out to me for anything. There will never be another us. I'm saving you now. Next time, I'm letting my man tear you a new asshole."

The way Mignon handled Javi had my dick rock hard. She could play that hard to get shit all she wanted to, but she was giving up the pussy tonight. It was time. No, I wasn't going to force her into doing something that she didn't want to do. At the same time, she needed to know that if she didn't want to be official with me and we weren't going to be fuckin', she couldn't press me about fuckin' other women. At the end of the day, I was a nigga that had needs and was used to a certain lifestyle. It was time for my drought to end.

Chapter Twenty-One:

Javi

"How'd your lil' date go?" Shawnte asked me as soon as I marched into the house.

"What date?" I asked.

"You had to have been somewhere since you weren't here with me and I know you weren't at anybody's job." She'd slipped up and told me that she knew where I was. Then she tried to play it off. I wasn't dumb. She'd just told on her damn self.

"It was you," I announced.

I moved towards her with my finger pointing in her face. Fear took over her body. I'm sure she was wondering if I were going to hit her or not. If she wasn't wondering, she needed to be worrying. The way I was feeling, anybody could catch these hands. At the same time, I knew that once I put my hands on her, there would be no coming back from that.

"You were the one who told Scorpio that I was meeting Mignon. How'd you find out about it?"

"Find out about what? I don't know what you're talking about," she lied.

"You can sit here and lie all you want, but I'm no damn fool. Why the fuck would you tell him that I was meeting up with her? Are you trying to get me killed or something?"

"Why would I try to get you killed? It's not like you have some insurance money that could take care of me and the baby if you were gone. I'd be a damn foo-," she stopped herself. "Do you have some money put back that I should know about?" she asked.

"If you needed to know about it, then you would know. I done told you about getting in my business. Everything ain't for you to know."

"Whelp, you might as well tell me since we see that little shit you tried to pull to get Mignon back didn't work." The sight of her laughing confirmed what I thought. She had to have gone through my phone and found out I was meeting with Mignon. What I didn't understand was how she could've gotten into my phone. I thought for sure I'd always been careful and concealed my passwords and any other important information from her. She was somebody that I didn't trust.

Shawnte was dumb. How was I so stupid and didn't see this before? Damn. I've always heard that sometimes you had to learn the hard way. If I would've known that this was going to be my hard way, I would've kept it moving.

"I'm not an idiot, Shawnte. I know you were the one that called Scorpio and told him that I was meeting up with Mignon. That was stupid as hell. You could've gotten me killed."

"I don't see the problem with that. I asked you to leave and you wouldn't. If he would've killed you, then I wouldn't have to worry about making you leave."

"You cold hearted as fuck, yo!"

"Naw. I'm just a nigga like you. Don't fuck over me and think I'm going to allow you to get away with it. Now, move out of my way so I can do a *Tik Tok*. You can do it with me if you want," she muttered.

Shawnte set her set up on the dresser and got in front of it. The stupidity in me thought she was joking until I heard a damn song playing.

"Down south, hood baby (Hood baby)
Make all the girls go crazy (Go crazy, go stupid)
Look up, down, to the side
Wok got me feeling lil' lazy
Shuffle (Shuffle), shuffle (Shuffle)"

The crazy broad really had the audacity to stop in the middle of a conversation to do a fuckin' *Tik Tok.* This couldn't be my life right now.

"Quit playing with me, Shawnte. How the hell you stop in the middle of a conversation to do a whole fuckin' *Tik Tok*? You need to take this shit seriously."

"For what? Life is too short to be serious all the time. You need to find you somebody else for all that. Somebody like Mignon's boring ass. Ain't that what you said? You liked to do things and all she ever wanted to do was work and sit in the house. That's funny because ever since I've been following her, she hasn't been sitting at the house. She'd go to work, be all in clubs, and riding dicks."

"Riding dicks? What the fuck are you talking about? She wouldn't dare give my pussy away," I grunted.

"Your pussy? You gave her dick away. Why get mad? Shit, that bitch decided it was best to cheat back," she laughed. The shit wasn't funny. Technically, it wasn't cheating because we weren't together, but it still felt wrong to me. I still felt as though she was betraying me. How was I supposed to get passed this shit?

Chapter Twenty-Two:

Mignon

How the hell did it go from me having the upper hand to the ball now being in Scorpio's court? We weren't even together so it wasn't like me going to hear Javi out was cheating. I told Scorpio to leave me alone anyway. I'm still trying to figure out how he knew that I was meeting up with Javi in the first place.

Here we were, sitting in his living room, not speaking. The silence between us was killing me. The only reason I hadn't said anything was because I was worried that he wasn't going to let me finish. That or he was going to say something that would crush my soul. I wanted to be very cautious with the way I moved around him.

After a good ten minutes of sitting there and him not even looking at me, I was really bothered. The shit was tearing me up inside. I hated for someone to be mad at me. Especially, when it was someone that I cared about. We hadn't been talking long, that much I knew. That didn't stop the fact that I'd began to develop strong feelings for him.

"Baby, will you at least look at me?" I got up from where I was sitting and went and sat in his lap. Positioning his arms to where they were wrapped around me, I was a little more at ease. He couldn't be that mad at me if he was allowing me to touch him. Right?

"What is it?" he quizzed, barely making eye contact with me.

"Look at me..." I softly touched the side of his face and turned it to where I could gaze into his eyes.

"I'm looking. What do you want?"

"Are you really that mad at me?"

"I'm mad about the whole situation. I know you had a right to be pissed off about what you thought happened between Aniya and me. You could've at least given me a chance to explain. Instead, you were so quick to run."

"I wasn't running. I needed to process things. It's not like you don't know what happened to me recently."

"Stop using that as a damn crutch. People get hurt every day. People fail at something every day. Does that mean you're supposed to stop living? Hell no."

"Who said I stopped living? I still live my life!"

"No, you shut down and are pretending to live life. You aren't happy and you and I both know that. I'm trying to give you the happiness I know that you're worth and you deserve but you're not letting me. That's hard on a nigga."

"It's only hard on you because you're so used to getting any and everything that you want. I'm not that chick that's going to fall to your knees and do everything that you request of me."

"Did I ask you to be that chick? Shit, I didn't even ask you to be mine."

"Oh, so you were just talking to me to get me comfortable enough to fuck me? That's fucked up and for that very reason, I'm glad that I didn't give you my pussy because it deserves way more than a nigga to be hunching on me like they the damn Energizer Bunny. My pussy ain't *NIKE*, you not finna *Just Do It*."

"It may not be *NIKE*, but the way that fat mufucka bustin' out through those pants, I bet that shit *Finger Lickin' Good* like *KFC*. You might as well quit playin' with a nigga and let me eat that shit until I get lockjaw."

I'm sure I was blushing my ass off. No man had ever said anything like that to me before. I wasn't going to be crazy and feed into it though. Everybody knows a man will say any and everything he can to get what he wants. That shit wasn't going to fly with me.

"Tell me why you were with Aniya and don't lie to me." I quickly changed the subject. If we continued to talk sexual to each other, then it was going to go down and I was trying to avoid it at all costs.

"Get up," he told me. Not waiting for him to tell me again, I stood, and he stood as well. He moved me around and sat me down in the chair before getting on his knees between my legs. That nigga was so tall that his face was still in front of mine. "I'm not going to lie to you. I've been bustin' pussies open since I was 14. Women throw their shit at me on a regular, so it ain't nothing for me to get some pussy. Fuckin' with you, I haven't been able to get none and beatin' my dick ain't what I'm on. I'm too old for that shit. We both grown and we both know what we doing so why not fuck? It's not like you don't want to and it's not like we not going to be together," he paused.

Scorpio dropped his head like he was gathering his thoughts. I didn't know if I should speak or wait for him to say something. What I did know was that he was rambling to me and not getting to what I wanted to know. Instead of saying something to make things worse between us, I decided to keep my mouth shut.

"I said all of that to say... When you deprive me and I'm horny, I have to get my needs met. Yes, I called Aniya over because I was familiar with her and I knew she'd come running. I didn't feel like going out and finding a new broad to deal with. When I called her over, we'd just gotten into it and I didn't know what was going to happen between us. It seemed to me that you had made up your mind about us not getting down and I didn't want to wait any longer. Did she suck my dick? Of course, she did. That didn't last long because I was ready to fuck something. In the midst of that, I couldn't go through with it. All I could think about was you. She got mad and we got into it when I told her to leave," he explained.

"You told her to leave?"

"Yeah, I did. Then she started acting all loud and ghetto. That was something I hated, which made shit worse. If you don't believe me, you can ask India."

"Who the fuck is India? There's another female I don't know about? Damn, were you about to have a threesome?" I sat up in the chair like I was about to do something to him while he laughed. "What's funny?" I asked. My face was all scrunched up.

"INDIA...." he hollered out and within a matter of minutes, another chick came running to the front of the house.

"Oh, hell no! I don't share. You not about to be fuckin' me and her at the same time," I exclaimed before jumping up. I almost hit him in the face with my knee. I was getting the hell away from him. He was crazy as hell if he thought I was about to be on some sister wives type shit.

Chapter Twenty-Three:

Scorpio

The way Mignon was acting could've made me pass out from laughter. She was doing too much. It was unreal how over dramatic she was being. If she even stopped and looked at India, she would've known that India wasn't my type. I liked females that were around my age or a little younger. India was old enough to be my mother, even though she was beautiful as hell. The only reason I hired her was because I knew I wouldn't be prone to sleep with her. I wasn't the type of man to shit where I slept.

"Chill out, ma. She's my housekeeper. India, this is Mignon. Mignon, this is..."

"India. Yeah, you told me. Sorry for tripping the way that I did. He has a problem with keeping his dick in his pants, so I thought you were somebody he was sleeping with too."

"You wouldn't have to worry about my dick being in my pants if you let me put it in you," I refuted. She glanced at me and rolled her eyes. The shit was mad annoying and cute at the same time.

"Whatever, I'm not going there with you."

"You are. I'm not even worried about it," I informed her. I turned and focused my attention on India before saying, "Can you please tell her what happened with Aniya the other day?" India rolled her eyes and sucked on her teeth. She never liked Aniya and I now knew why. I couldn't blame her for it because I didn't like her ass now either.

"She got upset and started hollering. You would've thought someone was killing her the way she was doing all of that damn screaming and hollering. Scorpio kept telling her to get out, but she acted like she didn't understand English. Then she answered the phone when you called so she could make you mad. Safe to say it worked. It worked in making you mad. It didn't work when it came to getting Scorpio to lay down with her. It only mad him madder and she was forced to get out. Trust me, nothing happened between the two of them," she explained.

"Told you. You have to trust me," I told Mignon.

"Trust you? Had you not thought about me then you would've kept going." I didn't want to tell her the real reason I stopped was because she started calling me. Had she not called me, my mind probably wouldn't have been on her and I would've still gotten it in. I guess it's true about the Lord working in mysterious ways.

"I told you that I was foul. There's nothing more that I can say. You can accept it or not. Either way, I know you're the woman for me. I want you but I'm not going to beg to keep you," I honestly spoke.

"Are you going to show me around or what?" Her changing the subject threw me for a loop. I scratched my head before excusing India and giving Mignon a tour around my palace. She had to have been amazed by all the 'Ohs' and 'Aws' coming from her mouth.

The last room I showed her was my bedroom. She acted like a kid by running over to my bed and getting on it. She stood up and started jumping like she'd lost her damn mind.

"Are you kiddin' me right now?" I asked, concerned that she was off her rocker.

"No. I've always wanted to jump in someone else's bed and since you owe me, I figured this was one way you could repay me," she expressed.

"One way? What's another way because this right here ain't working for me?" I chided, pointing my finger at her jumping up and down. She stopped jumping and giggled before pointing a finger at me and motioning for me to move closer to her. It took me a minute to do. I had to make sure she wasn't on no revenge type shit and was going to try to hit me or something. Yeah, I've had women brave enough to try me like that before. Let's just say, they won't be trying anybody else that way.

"What's up, ma?" I asked when I got to the end of the bed.

"I don't want my pussy to be vegan anymore. Feed her some of this meat," she requested, rubbing on my dick through my pants. My body already had a mind of its own when it came to her so her rubbing my dick didn't make matters any better. I instantly bricked up as she continued to rub on it. I stuck my hands out and began to caress her breast. They were beautiful as fuck. I could tell that by seeing the way they sat up in her shirt. I couldn't wait to see how they would be when I'd gotten her naked.

My head dropped back from the pleasure I was receiving from just her touch alone. The sound of my zipper coming undone caused me to peer up at her. She had a smirk on her face as if she was telling me, "I got this. Enjoy what

I'm about to do to you." She didn't have to say a word. I planned on giving her free range to do any and everything that she wanted to do to me. My dick was fully erect.

"Your dick is so pretty, baby. I've been waiting to taste it," she said just before slithering it inside of her mouth. She allowed it to swim in her mouth before she pulled it out, kissed the tip, and started massaging my balls. It was feeling so good that my legs began to feel weak. I had to place my hand on her shoulders to keep from losing my balance.

"Fuck! Suck that shit, ma," I commented. Without doubt, she stuck it back inside her mouth. All the saliva she had built up mixed with the warmth of her mouth was driving me crazy. I couldn't take it anymore. I had to feel the inside of her. "Take that shit off," I told her, ordering her to take her clothes off. She stood from where she was and removed every article of clothing that covered her body. The glow of her skin was everything I'd expected and more. She was gorgeous. "Lay down," I instructed her.

With Mignon lying on the bed butt booty ass naked, I crawled between her legs. Placing each leg on one of my shoulders, my tongue came out of my mouth and dipped inside of her love tunnel. Her pussy was sweeter than honey. As my tongue found a new home inside of her fat juicy pussy, the juices from her pussy made its way down to her ass. I took one of my fingers and moved it around in the spit to get it moist before inserting that finger inside of her asshole.

The way her body jumped when I touched her let me know I was doing a good job at pleasing her. That was all I ever wanted to do since the moment I first laid eyes on her.

"I'm finna cum," she announced.

"You better hold that shit in. We don't cum unless we cumin' together," I told her.

"I can't hold it. I'm about to cu-" I pulled back thinking if I moved my mouth, I'd be able to stop her from reaching her peak, but that didn't work. The moment I'd pulled away from her, she shot her juices everywhere. Her body began to jerk and convulse. It scared me when her eyes rolled to the back of her head. "Fuckkkk...." she yelled.

"You okay, ma?" I asked, seriously worried about her.

"I'm good. All I need is some dick in my life now," she stated. She didn't have to say that shit again. Swiftly, I got between my legs and attempted to slide inside of her. She wasn't lying when she said she hadn't been with anybody. That was evidenced by her pussy being virgin tight. It took me a minute, but once I got in there, I was good. I laid there for a while to allow her to adjust to my size. Having a big dick was both a blessing and a curse.

"You tight as fuck, ma."

"I know. I've been waiting for someone like you to come in my life and show me what it's like to get some real dick," she admitted. I chuckled at her talking shit.

Stroking inside of Mignon, all kinds of thoughts crossed my mind. I was falling for her and hard. It hadn't been long since we'd been talking. However, I'd been watching her for a while. The first time I laid eyes on her, I wanted her. Now, I was having to deal with controlling my feelings. While she was worried about herself getting hurt, I was worried about me. Love is a two-way street. There's no way she could think if something went wrong between us, she would be the only one suffering behind it.

"I'm about to cum again," she announced. I was so caught off in my thoughts that I hadn't been doing my job. I quickly pulled out of her. She looked at me like she wanted to kill me. She had to understand that I wanted to nut at the same time as her.

"We nutting together and I'm not ready yet. That means you have to hold that shit in." She nodded her head in understanding.

Quickening my pace, I started delivering long, deep strokes to her. Mignon's soft moans got louder and louder. She began screaming my name and her legs began shaking uncontrollably. She was about to explode and so was I.

"Here it cum, ma," I told her as I painted her insides with my seeds.

"I'm cumin' too, baby," she said, and her shaking became more intense. She started mumbling and saying shit I didn't understand. It was like she was speaking in tongues. I didn't want to pull out of her, but I knew I had to. If I didn't and my dick woke up again, she was going to be in for a rude awakening.

Mignon rolled over to her side and put her thumb in her mouth. I laughed. She didn't bother to get up to clean herself up or nothing.

"You good, ma?"

"I'm great. You good?"

"I'm a tad bit hungry. Can you go make me a sandwich or something? I requested.

"If I can get up and make a sandwich or even walk a step right now, that means you didn't do your job and there would be no repeat of you getting this good good," she quipped. I couldn't even argue with her. Instead, I nestled up under her and we just laid there.

Chapter Twenty-Four:

Aniya

I'd been hiding in Scorpio's closet waiting to bust out and profess my love to him. I was also going to be the bigger woman and apologize for talking crazy about Mignon. That was until I saw him walking in his bedroom with her. It seemed like he was only letting her check the house out. I wasn't expecting them to start fuckin'. She was a bigger woman than me, but her skin was flawless. She was actually beautiful.

Watching him dive inside of her turned me on. I sat on the floor with my legs Indian style, peeking through the crack in the door. Licking my fingers, I began dipping them in and out of my pussy. I used my thumb to massage my clit. The pleasure intensified when Mignon's moans grew louder. I wanted desperately to go join them. Maybe if Scorpio saw that I could be a team player, he'd let both of us stick around and not just Mignon. I was desperate. I was willing to do anything at this point.

When Scorpio announced he was about to cum, I'd reached my climax and was cumin' too. One thing about him, he was going to make sure you received just as much pleasure as him, if not more.

"Don't stop, baby. I'm cumin' too. Keep fuckin' that bitch. Go deep in that muthafuckin' pussy and make that bitch scream," I softly said as I sped up my pace. I rubbed on my clit so fast and hard, I almost sparked a fire. Next thing I knew, my body flew back as my juices went flying everywhere. On his clothes, shoes, walls, and even on the closet door. That was his fault though. He shouldn't have been fuckin' her so damn good.

Jerking one of his shirts down, I used it to wipe up as much of my mess as I could.

"You ready for round two?" The closet door flew open and Scorpio just stared at me.

"How'd you know I was in here?"

"I heard you breathing, and I heard that loud as noise you like to make when you bust one. Why the fuck you in my closet, watching me with my girl?"

"I didn't know she was going to be here. I honestly thought I could come back here, and we could talk."

"How'd you get in?"

"I never gave my key back and you never changed the locks." What I say that for? He put his hand out for me to put the key in it. I was too scared to tell him no. He'd probably fuck me up for real. Without hesitation, I placed the key in his hand and rose from the floor. Backing away from him, I managed to lock eyes with Mignon who was running full force towards me. Scorpio caught her right as she was about to punch me.

"Chill out, baby. She's not worth it."

"Not worth it? You wasn't saying that when I was suckin' your dick."

"I didn't have to tell you then. I've told you plenty of times before," he nonchalantly spoke.

"Why are you treating me like this? I didn't mean to cheat on you. I didn't mean to hurt you. What is it going to take for you to forgive me?" I pleaded with him. I missed Scorpio and hated the way he was acting towards me. "Let me fix this."

"There is no fixing it. You got a better chance at killing yourself than to ever feel this dick again," Mignon muttered, grabbing ahold of Scorpio's dick. They both stood before me naked.

"Let's have a threesome. You remember you used to love those, baby? Me, you, and Mignon can all have a threesome right now," I suggested before starting to remove my clothes.

"Bitch, I don't share. Take your thirsty ass on somewhere with that dumb shit," she fussed. "I'm going to clean myself up. She needs to be gone when I make it back from the bathroom or we're done," she told him.

Scorpio kept his eyes trained on me. I'm sure he was thinking I had a lot of balls to break into his house. I couldn't help it. I was willing to go above and beyond to prove to him that I was sorry for what I'd done and that I really wanted to work things out. As we stood there in dead silence, Scorpio suddenly fell out laughing.

His laughter took me away from my thoughts. I licked my lips and glanced down at his dick. He realized what I was doing and seemingly became uncomfortable. He scanned the room with his eyes before walking away from me. He picked up his boxers and proceeded to put them on.

"On second thought... You don't have to worry about her leaving, I'm going to help her ass." Mignon came running out of the bathroom with a sling blade in her hand.

"No, baby. Remember what you told me earlier? She's not worth it. Let's just let her leave."

"She'll leave after I dangle her out the window by her damn feet. She trying the right one."

"Ain't nobody scared of you. I can handle myself," I bellowed. The thought of fighting her wasn't my issue. I've always been told that when someone barks loud, they have a small bite. She was barking loud as hell right now so I knew I could take her.

"You can handle her?" Scorpio quizzed.

"You heard what I said," I repeated.

"Fine by me. Do your thang, baby," he told her as he let her go.

Mignon came charging at me like a bull. Before I could react, she'd hit me with a three-piece combo that had me dizzy as fuck. I started swinging my arms like I was about to take flight, not connecting with anything. Every swing Mignon took connected with some part of my body. I could hear Scorpio in the background laughing. The shit must've lasted for ten minutes before he did anything to stop it.

"Let her make it, baby. If she hits you, we are going to have a problem. I'm not risking you losing my seed," he remarked.

My eyes grew big as hell. He never wanted to have children when we were together. He kept saying it wasn't the right time. He wanted to stack his paper and get out of the street shit before we brought a child into this world. So, I knew damn well he wasn't about to let her have his child. What was so good about her? What made her so much different and better than me? That was something I'd never be able to understand.

"Seed? What damn seed? We only had sex one time and that was tonight," she replied. That caused my tension to ease a bit. It made me feel better that he was just talking to hear himself talk or to make me feel bad.

"I know that I got that ass pregnant tonight. That shit was too fuckin' good. I don't think I've ever had any pussy that good before in my life," he bragged.

"Stop with the bullshit. I know you're saying that to piss me off and it's not going to work," I commented.

"Is she still standing here? I know she not still standing there," Mignon spoke.

"I'm out," I told them. Gathering my belongings, I hightailed it out of the room. That was the best thing for me. The longer I would've stayed up there, the worse things would've become. I couldn't afford to be fucked up or killed by Scorpio. Even though I left, that didn't mean I was giving up. They would both be seeing me again. Bet that.

Chapter Twenty-Five:

Scorpio

(One Month Later...)

"Wait... What happened? Say that shit again so I'll know I heard you correctly."

"It's some money coming up short. Then the niggas responsible for the money missing too."

"How much is missing?"

"A little over $250,000," Twist stated.

"Fuck you mean? How the hell did that even happen?" I roared.

"Link up with me so we can talk about this. You know damn well we don't discuss this type of shit over the phone," Twist reminded me.

Being so irate at what he'd said to me, I completely forgot that we were on the phone. I was sitting in the bed enjoying my time with my baby when all of a sudden Twist hit my line and told me some money was missing.

"Baby, I have to go link up with Twist. Why don't you call Robin over and ya'll go do something? Maybe swing by your place and start packing up your shit so you can come back here," I commented to Mignon.

"Do what? Pack it up for what?" she curiously asked.

"For the past two months, we've been inseparable. I've gotten used to you being around all the time. You see even when you try to go home, I make up a reason for you to stay or I go with you. I don't want you by yourself. I want to be under you at all times," I admitted. Call it soft or whatever you want to call it, but I knew I was in love. Mignon was it for me. In a few more months, depending on how things went, I was more than prepared to make things real official by asking her to be my wife.

"Are you asking me to move in with you?"

"I'm not asking you anything. I'm telling you that I want you to move in with me. What's it going to hurt if we're living together?"

"What if we break up? What will I have to go back to? What if we get into a big fight and need some space? I wouldn't want to be in your presence at all."

"Why are you being so negative right now? Have I given you a reason to doubt that we would be together?"

"You have three reasons why I think we might not be together and all three of them is hanging between your legs," she muttered, trying to be funny. It wasn't a joke. She picked the wrong time to try to be funny.

"Mannnn... Watch out! I'm not doing this with you. Every time we have a problem, you revert back to what happened between you and Javi. I told you I wasn't him. I would never do to you what he did. I've never used you or asked you for anything other than to be with me."

"And I'm with you. I'm just not ready to move in with you."

"Aight. Bet."

"Bet? Oh, you saying you bout to find somebody else to move in with you?"

"Is that what came out of my mouth? You hear what you want to hear."

"No. I'm speaking from experience with you. When you didn't want to wait to be with me, I had to deal with you being with Aniya's ass. You got that free pass, it won't happen again," she warned me. At that point, I was over it. We were a little over two months in and she was still dwelling on things from the past. She was either going to keep dwelling on the shit and stay in the past or forgive me and move the fuck on.

"Mignon, I love you and I'm willing to do almost anything that I have to do to make things go right between us."

"Almost anything, what is almost?"

"I'm not going to deal with you continuously bringing up shit that happened between us in the past. You claim you forgave me for it, then let the shit go. You're not going to be throwing it in my face every damn chance you get. Another thing is that you're going to quit bringing up Javi and what he did to you. I'm not him. In the time that we've talked, I've never given you a reason to think I was going to use and abuse you. If you can't do that then we don't need to be together," I explained. There was no way I was going to keep tolerating the fact that she can't let go of the past. "Everybody is not out to get you," I expressed.

"I didn't say you were out to get me. I'm hurt and I'm trying to heal from it. Maybe getting into this relationship with you happened too soon. I think we need to take a break," she stated. I was stunned. What the fuck was she even talking about?

"If I would've known that expressing to you that I wanted us to live together would've ended with us breaking up, then I never would've said anything."

"I didn't say we were breaking up. All I'm asking for is a little break." She tried her best to recover from what she was saying.

"I'm going to say this one time and one time only because I'm supposed to be dealing with something else. You're my woman and you're supposed to be my peace. If you disturb my peace, then we have a problem and that's exactly what you're doing right now. If you want a break, then that's perfectly fine. Will it hurt me? Yeah, it will. Will it stop me from living my life? No, it will not."

"So, what you're saying is that you're going to get another bitch?"

"That's not what I was saying at all and it's sad that was all you got from what I said to you. You need to know that if we are on a break then there is no reason for you to worry about who I'm with or what I'm doing." Without giving her a chance to respond, I grabbed what I needed and left.

The whole time I was driving to get to Twist, Mignon was blowing my phone up. There was no reason for me to answer. She said what she wanted to happen between us, and I wasn't going to argue with her. Like I've said before, one thing I was not was the cops. There wasn't a single soul paying me to chase and cuff her mufuckin' ass. If she wanted to be on that childish shit, then I was going to let her have it. She was just going to have to be on it without me.

Chapter Twenty-Six:

Mignon

Scorpio had lost his mind. How the hell did he think it was okay for him to get mad at me for not wanting to move in with him? Yeah, we'd been together for a minute. That's all it was... a MINUTE. There was no way that we were ready to live together when we were getting into fights practically every other damn day.

One thing I could admit to was that most of the fights happened to be my fault. There was so much that I needed to change within myself. The therapist that I'd been seeing since everything happened between Javi and I told me that. I was always guarded and had built a wall up because I wanted to avoid being hurt again. Yet, the wall that I built up was the reason I was being hurt. Not allowing Scorpio to get close to me only made things worse. It showed that I didn't trust him. How could we be in a relationship if I wasn't fully ready to trust him and give him my heart?

Asking him for a break was the only thing I could think of to keep him from wanting to move in together right now. He seemed to not understand when I would tell him that I was scared of us moving so fast in our relationship. He did whatever he could to assure me that he wouldn't hurt me and that he was going to do whatever he could to make me happy, but I didn't trust him enough to believe that. Even when he did do something for me, I often made the situation a bad one because I would question why he was doing it.

I'd repeatedly called his phone hoping he would answer so that we could talk about things further, but he kept sending me to voicemail. He was mad at me and I got that. That wasn't enough for him to ignore me. What happened to communicating in your relationship? How can we make things right if he didn't communicate?

Calling him once more, I was hurt and annoyed that he didn't answer. Luckily, I'd had some clothes lying around from staying over there for weeks. I laughed at myself when I stepped inside the closet. Scorpio called himself rearranging his closet so that I would have my own space. He even had someone bring a whole dresser in so that I would have additional space.

The more I stood there thinking about things, the more I realized how stupid I was. Scorpio was right when he talked about all the time we'd spent together. I'd basically been living with him already. It was just not something that we acknowledged. Him talking about it today made me nervous. I thought things were fine the way that they were. The minute we started changing things was when things were going to start getting bad between us. That's the way things always happened. That's what scared me the most. I was falling for him. Forget was. I had fallen for him. HARD!

"Wait a minute... Did he say that he loved me?" I asked myself. It was sad that I was so worried about things going wrong that I completely overlooked the fact that he told me he loved me. I was such a damn fool.

Knowing that I had to make things right, I searched the room for my phone. When I got it, I called the only other person I knew I could trust.

"Hello..." Robin answered on the second ring.

"What you doing?"

"I was waiting on Twist to come over, but he told me that he had to meet up with Scorpio. He said something about their money being stolen or something."

"Do you know where they went?"

"I think they went to meet up at one of their little meeting spots. They change them up so much, you never know which one they go to."

"Do you know where any of those spots are?"

"I think I know three of them. I've rode with Twist a few times and somewhat eavesdropped on their conversations. Why? What's wrong?"

"Get dressed, bitch. I'm on my way!" I told her before ending the call. There was no reason for me to wait on her to respond. I was not about to give her the chance to tell me no.

Tossing clothes out of my drawers, I put on some black tights with a black cami and a black sweater. Thank God I had my black Timbs to wear too. Dressed down in all black, I locked up the house and hopped in my car. Making it to Robin's house in no time, she came out wearing some bright red shit. I had to make her go back in the house and change. She was fussing, which was understandable, but she still changed her clothes.

"What the fuck is going on? Why the hell did I need to be in all black?" she questioned me.

"I may have messed things up with Scorpio and now I have to find a way to fix them." That was all I was telling her. She didn't need to know the details because that was only going to make her laugh at me and that wasn't going to make things any better.

"You couldn't have called him on the phone?" she asked.

"Don't you think I tried that first? His ass won't answer any of my calls," I explained.

"Maybe he was busy. I told you that him and Twist had some business to handle."

"I appreciate you trying to remain positive and what not, but that nigga not answering any of my calls. I started calling him right when he let the house. That lets me know that he's ignoring me on purpose. You know how much I hate being ignored."

"Yeah, don't we all know it. If he didn't know it before, he was surely going to know tonight," she giggled. I laughed with her because she was giving straight facts.

Robin and I drove around to the three spots she could remember. We were unsuccessful at each location. When we were about to leave the last spot, a black car zoomed past us. It looked like one of Scorpio's many cars. Since I didn't pay attention to the one he left the house in, I decided to follow the car. It couldn't possible hurt anything.

"Slow down, don't get too close on the car," Robin told me.

"I know what I'm doing, Robin."

"No, the fuck you don't. If you did, we wouldn't be following behind an unknown car. You don't know if that's Scorpio or not."

Instead of responding to her, I kept my eyes trained on the car. We trailed it for at least 15 minutes before he turned into some apartment complex. It wasn't one that I'd been to before, but I knew that it was a bad complex because it was always on the news and people were constantly talking about it.

The car came to a sudden stop on side of the road. Slowing down, I pulled over behind it. In my opinion, I was far enough behind it to where he couldn't see me.

"What are you doing? You're too close," Robin warned me once more.

"No, I'm not. I know what I'm doing." It sounded better in my mind than it did when it came out of my mouth. We both knew I didn't have a clue in hell what I was doing. This was something new to me. My mind raced thinking of what I should do next. It caught me off guard when Scorpio jumped out of the car in front of us and marched towards me. Twist wasn't too far behind him.

"Oooohhhhh... Bitch, you in trouble," Robin called herself teasing me.

"Oooohhhhh... Your damn self because here comes Twist's ass too," I told her. She froze up like she'd seen a ghost. I couldn't help but laugh at her. I'd never seen a man have her so scared. Hell, I'd never seen a man that had her all to himself either. My girl was known for being a man eater. They didn't stand a chance with her.

Boom... Boom... Boom...

Scorpio beat on my car window. I kept my head forward because I was too scared to look at him.

"Open this fuckin' door, Mignon. I know you see and hear me," he roared.

Hesitantly, I opened the door. I wondered why he didn't tell me to let the window down instead. I quit wondering as soon as he snatched my ass out the car and pinned me up against it.

"Please, don't hurt me. I'm sorry." I clammed up in fear. The expression on his face fucked with me. It was one I'd never be able to erase.

"What the hell are you doing, Mignon? Why are you following me?"

"I'm not following you. We just so happen to be going in the same direction," I lied.

"Oh word?"

"Yeah. See, you worried for nothing."

"Where you going then?"

"Huh?" Damn. I should've been faster on my feet. Scorpio got on my damn nerves being so nosey.

"Huh, my ass. Where are you going, Mignon?"

"I don't ask you where you're going, so why are you asking me? I'm grown, Scorpio."

"You right. You grown, ma. Do you."

For some reason, my heart dropped to my feet. Was he breaking up with me? I'd learned him well enough to know he didn't drop shit that easily. What had changed? Had he stopped caring about me? What the fuck was going on?

"Are you breaking up with me?"

"Naw. You broke up with yourself, ma. I'm out. Go handle your business," he told me.

My face hit the ground. He walked away from me and all I could do was stand there. I was worried sick. Was he really done with me? That was the only thing I could think about. The shit was crazy. What had I done that was so bad for him to walk away from me for good?

Chapter Twenty-Seven:

Scorpio

Nobody couldn't tell me that I didn't love Mignon. I did. I loved her more than I loved any other woman on this earth. I loved her more than the money I made. If she would've asked me at some point to walk away from this street shit, then I would.

"Hol' up, man," Twist called behind me as he jogged to catch up with me.

"What?" I roared.

"Take that bass out of your voice with me. I'm trying to figure out what the fuck is going on. Why you tripping on her like that?"

"Mind your business, Twist. You need to be worried about Robin being out here with her."

"I talked to Robin. She told me that Mignon was coming to make shit right with you. I'm sure you scared the hell out of her by the way you hopped your King Kong looking ass out the car and stormed towards her. If I were a bitch, I'd be scared too."

"I don't have time to worry about that right now. We need to get to this meeting to figure out what the hell is going on with our money."

"That shit can wait. You said you loved her. If you really love her, then you need to make this shit right with her. Look at her standing over there looking goofy as fuck." Twist chuckled. That caused me to glance over at her.

"She do look silly as fuck, huh?" We both started laughing at the shit. "Fine, I'll go over there and talk to her but if she on some bullshit, it's a wrap," I warned him.

"I hear ya, man. Everything's going to be all good."

Twist and I headed in the direction of Mignon's car. Out of nowhere, a set of headlights came flying towards us.

"GET IN THE CAR!" I hollered at Mignon.

"You don't tell me what to do, Scorpio. I told you that I was grown. Stop acting like you're my father and you're running things because you certainly are not," she fussed.

"GET YOUR ASS IN THE CAR NOWWWWWWW!" I roared. That still wasn't enough to convince her.

"Run, nigga. If she wanna stand her ditzy ass up there arguing, let her argue with this fuckin' air. This shit suspect as fuck," Twist stated before taking off towards the car to take cover.

There was no way I could leave Mignon standing out there. Twist was right. Something about this shit seemed suspect as hell. I took off running in the direction of Mignon as the car neared me.

RATATATATAT... RATATATAT... RATATATAT...

Bullets rang out. It was coming from the car. There was nowhere for me to run or anywhere for me to take cover where I wouldn't be hit. The distance between my car and Mignon's car left too much of an open playing field. I was fucked. I tried to run towards Twist, who was busting back, but I didn't get there fast enough.

All I felt was my skin burning and tearing as the bullets hit me. The shit was unreal. As long as I'd been in the game, I'd never been caught slipping like this. I'd never been shot. Shot at, yes. Shot, no! None of the shit made sense. All of this bad shit started happening when I allowed Mignon to enter my life. Had she set me up? That was the only explanation I came up with.

The car zoomed by and the gunfire ceased. I laid on the ground in one of the most awkward positions I'd ever been in, fighting for my life.

"Call 9-1-1!" I heard Twist say.

"Nooooo... Nooooo... Nooooo... This can't be happening. God, please cover Scorpio. I love him so much. Don't take him away from me," Mignon kneeled over me crying. If I could move, I'd knock her in her shit. If she would've listened to me instead of standing there wanting to bitch and fuss over bullshit, then I would've been straight. This had to be my sign from God that although I wanted her for me, she wasn't the one. That was cool because after this shit that she pulled tonight, I was on some "Fuck, Mignon," type shit and there was nothing anybody could say or do to change that.

Chapter Twenty-Eight:

Javi

"It's done." Hearing those words were like music to my ears. Yeah, I could've taken Scorpio out myself, but it felt so much better getting someone else to do it. It made me feel like I was in control all over again.

With Scorpio out of the way, I could be there for Mignon. Help her mourn and heal from her lose. With me being there every step of the way while she grieved, that meant that we'd grow closer and I'd have my chance of being with her again.

Yeah, I heard her loud and clear when she said she didn't want to be with me because of what I'd done to her. Do you think I believed that? Hell no. Shit, you probably didn't even believe the shit yourself.

"What the hell you smiling for?" Shawnte stepped in the room with me and asked.

"Nothing that concerns you," I replied.

"Why must you always be an asshole?"

"Why must you always nag me? We said we wasn't fuckin' with each other on that level anymore, so you might as well get out of my face. I've been on my grind non-stop to find my way back up to the top. Now that I've found out how I was going to do it, there really is no reason for me to stick around here with you," I told her.

"Good. I don't know how many more times I can tell you to get lost anyways," she rattled off.

"Whatever. I'm not going to argue with you. You do your thing and I'll do mine."

"So, it's okay for me to fuck another nigga? I need to make sure. That way I don't have to worry about your coming at me wrong about it later."

"It's not like you aren't already doing it," I commented. One thing I wasn't when it came to Shawnte, was a fool. She had no problem sleeping with any man that could throw money her way. I knew that from experience. If I wasn't sending her the money Mignon had been sending me, then we wouldn't be where we were now.

"What is that supposed to mean?"

"Nothing. Where's my son at?" I asked.

"After all this time, you just now want to ask about your son?"

"I don't care when I asked about him. You need to tell me where he is so we can go get him," I demanded.

"He's been living with my mother," she informed me.

"Living with her? What you mean? You told me that he would stay the night with her from time to time. Is that why he hasn't been around?" Shawnte got quiet. That wasn't like her, so I knew she was trying to think of a lie. "Don't start lying to me either. Where is my son?" I raised my voice.

"Don't yell at me," she cowardly replied.

"Don't tell me not to yell at you if you can't produce my seed. I'm not about to play with your ass. You need to give me answers and I want them now." She started moving her feet around like she was playing in sand. The more she stood there looking stupid, the more she was pissing me off. It was crazy how we had a child together that I barely saw and whenever I asked her about him, she had a different answer as to where he was. Why didn't I think about all of this before today? It had me questioning if the child was even mine.

When Shawnte first told me about being pregnant, I was mad. I wanted her to go get an abortion. If Mignon would've found out about the baby, she would've left me. In my mind, the only way to keep my seed a secret was if I was able to get Shawnte to get rid of it. I wasn't ready for children and neither was she. However, she looked at it differently. It was a meal ticket for her. She kept the baby and convinced me that the best thing for us was to be a family. Since I thought I loved her, I went along with what I wanted.

Looking back at it, I was the prime example of a man not doing right by the good woman he had at home. I stepped out on my relationship and allowed Shawnte to have me thinking that being with her would be the better fit for me. I see differently now. If I would've known then what I knew now, there was no way in hell I'd be where I was. I'd still be with Mignon, living my best life.

Mignon wasn't a dime by any means, she wasn't ugly either. When I first met her, she was very petite. As our relationship progressed, she started gaining weight. I stayed with her because I didn't want her to think I was shallow. She hadn't changed as a person, only in her appearance. That was enough for me to not be attractive to her anymore. I also stayed with her because she knew how to take care of a man. She spoiled me. The things that a man should do for a woman, she did for me. Don't start tripping though because I did for her to. She started going to school because of me. I encouraged her when she wanted to give up. I wasn't nowhere near the crappy boyfriend to her that people think. If I was, she would've left me a long time ago. Trust me! Mignon loved me to the core, but she wouldn't have dealt with anything more than she thought she could handle. Why you think she was so loyal and faithful to me? She stuck around after I cheated twice so I couldn't tell her about Shawnte until I knew for sure that I was ready to be done with our relationship.

From the time I got locked up, Mignon rode hard for me. Yet, Shawnte was there too. Mignon took care of me financially. That made me feel somewhat less of a man. Shawnte stroked my ego and made me still feel like I was running shit. She seemed like my rock at that point. Sounds dumb as hell now that I'm thinking about everything. A nigga fucked up bad and trust me, I was paying for it royally.

"You don't hear me talking to you?" Shawnte yelled, removing me from my thoughts.

"If you not talking to me about what I want to know, then you don't need to be talking to me about shit. Where is my son?" I questioned again. This time through clenched teeth.

"I need to tell you something," she sheepishly spoke.

"Don't try to use that childlike, shy voice with me. I don't have all day for this. You better start talking and it better be what I want to hear or we're going to have some serious problems."

"Fine. There's no reason for me to continue to lie to you so open your ears and listen to me good. I will not repeat myself. Right after I had him, I left him in the car by himself so I could run inside the store. I only went in to get one thing. While I was in there, I ended up seeing some cute little outfits for him. I got so sidetracked that I completely forgot about him being in the car and someone ended up calling the police on me. The Department of Family and Children's Services came in and took him away from me. They gave custody to my mother since she was the closest relative that I had. He never came to any of the visits with me because I only had supervised visits. That meant I'd have to bring my mother with me to see you and that wasn't going to work."

The shit was unreal. Why didn't I see how trifling she was from the jump? I already felt like she'd gotten pregnant on purpose. Since I didn't have the proof of it, I never said anything about it. The more she talked the more I felt as though she trapped me. She saw me in the streets on a come up and because she was tired of living that poor ass lifestyle she was living before we got together, she made sure I got her pregnant. That was a damn shame. Why the fuck try to keep someone with a baby? I must say she played it well. She wanted to trap me and that's exactly what she was able to do.

"Let me get this straight... You used my baby as a pawn to get me to be with you when all this time, you never even had custody of him? Who does stupid ass shit like that? What if I would've told you that I still didn't want to be with you after you told me you were pregnant?"

"You may be an asshole from time to time. But you have a heart of gold when it comes to children. I knew that from seeing you interact with some of the neighborhood kids. So, if you had one of your own, I knew that you were going to go above and beyond to make sure the baby was good. That meant to me that as long as my baby was good, then I'd be good," she emphasized. She was right though. Kids were near and dear to me. I didn't have it good growing up. Whenever I saw a child in need, I'd go out of my way to make sure they were straight.

"I'm not doing this with you. I understand that you wanted a child. Trapping me was not the way to do it. Besides it's not like it worked out in your favor anyways. You didn't come up off me. You are still the same struggling bitch that I met years ago," I muttered.

"Fuck you, Javi! Say what you want about me. I bet me and my baby are going to be alright."

"Your baby? Bitch go get my son. It's about time that he started living with me."

"You're not taking my son anywhere."

"Your son? You haven't been a mother to him since he's been on this earth so don't try that 'my son' shit with me. Go get him or I'll go get him myself. I can promise you that you don't want me approaching your mother."

Shawnte stared at me with a snide smirk on her face. She didn't budge. It was almost as if she took me as a joke.

"Fine. I got this," I told her as I jumped up to go get dressed.

"Where do you think you're going? I know you're not about to go over to my mother's house and start some shit. She already doesn't like you. She doesn't even have anything to do with all this mess going on between us."

"She has everything to do with this if my son is there with her when he should be here with me. You think I care that she don't like me? I don't like that baldheaded scaly wag either. At this point, I'm tired of giving you the option of bringing him home. I'll go get my son my damn self."

"HE'S NOT YOUR SON," she blurted out. Surely, I didn't hear her correctly. Did she just tell me that the little boy that was my namesake wasn't mine? There was no way that was what I heard from her.

"What did you just say to me?"

"You heard what I said. He's not your son, Javi."

"If he's not my son, then whose son is he?" Shawnte became quiet. She was never quiet. "Don't get quiet now. You've always had so much that you wanted to say. Open your mouth and tell me who the fuck is the father of your son."

"TWIST! Twist is the father. Are you happy now?" she screamed.

Before I knew it, I was on top of Shawnte banging her head on the floor. How could she do this to me? Why did she hurt me when all I wanted to do was give her the world? It wasn't my fault that things weren't going the way that we planned for them to go. That didn't make me less of a man. I always thought our time was coming. All she had to do was stand by a nigga, have my back, and remain loyal and everything her heart desired would be hers. She fucked that up. It was then that I realized how Mignon felt when I hurt her.

Chapter Twenty-Nine:

Mignon

"This is all my fault."

"This is not your fault, boo. We all happened to be in the wrong place at the wrong time. Any of us could have been hit." Robin was trying her best to help me feel better.

"Could have been but weren't. What if he dies? I'll never be able to live with myself. If I would've listened to him then he would've been in his car far away from where we were."

"I keep telling you that it isn't your fault. Whomever it was had to have been out to get him. If they didn't get him tonight, they would've gotten him some other time. You can't control an idiot with a gun. Right now, you need to calm down and get yourself together. Scorpio is going to need you."

"What if he decides he doesn't want anything else to do with me? It's not like I can blame him because I was wrong. This hurts so much. I don't want to lose him," I cried. Robin pulled me into her arms like a mother nurturing her child.

"Calm down, boo. Everything is going to be okay. Scorpio is going to be okay. He's going to bounce back so fast that you won't know what hit you."

"Stop telling her this ain't her fault because it is her damn fault. My nigga let his guard down and allowed her in. He fell in love with her and when he needed her hardheaded ass to listen, she wanted to be on that baldheaded hoe shit. That's that fuck shit and if my dude don't make it, I'm putting a bullet in that bitch's skull," he threatened.

"Don't do that, baby. You acted like we knew this was going to happen," Robin tried to reason with him.

"How the fuck am I supposed to feel? Y'all following our every move and shit. Then this shit pops off. He gets hit and y'all don't."

"Why the fuck you keep saying y'all like I had somebody shooting at him?" Robin asked.

"Cuz y'all in this shit together. How the fuck am I supposed to know that you weren't apart of some fucked up scheme with her? He did decide he no longer wanted to be with her bougie ass. She probably tried to have him taken out so he couldn't give his dick and money to the next bitch."

"Do you even hear yourself right now? I've never given you a reason to not trust me," Robin fussed. She was furious and I couldn't blame her. Twist was blaming her for something that was solely my fault.

"This isn't her fault, Twist. If you're going to blame somebody than that somebody needs to be me. I was the one in the wrong. He wasn't answering my calls so I decided I would pop up on him."

"You can't make no damn body talk to your ass," Twist hollered. "I see why Javi did you the way that he did. You don't deserve my nigga. Get the fuck on. Neither one of you bitches is wanted around here," he barked and left us standing in the waiting room looking crazy.

"Does that mean you aren't going to call me and let me know how he's doing?" I stupidly asked. Twist glanced back at me with a look of death on his face. I knew then that my best bet was to shut my fuckin' mouth.

"Come on, sis. We will get this shit worked out," I commented to Robin.

"Sis, my ass. I told you not to do this shit. You never listen. I told you Javi wasn't the one for you, but you had to fuck him anyways. You gave that nigga the world and he shitted on you. Why? Because you didn't listen to me. I told you that Scorpio was a good man and that you needed to open yourself up to him. Did you listen? Fuck no! You got mad at him over some dumb shit. Do you not know that most street niggas be slanging their dicks to any bitch that thy can while their bitch sitting at home worried about them? Scorpio never done that to you. Hell, he stepped away from the street shit so he could spend more time with you. How do I know? Twist told me. Now, he in there fighting for his life because you couldn't get your shit together. I understand Javi hurt you, but that doesn't mean you allow your life to go down in flames and take the people who love you with you," Robin snapped. She was right. There was no denying that.

"I'm sorry," I called myself apologizing.

"I'm not trying to hear that shit. The only reason you're apologizing is because I went off on your ass. Had I not said anything, you wouldn't have even opened your mouth to speak on the situation. I know you feel like you didn't do anything wrong and that's your right to feel that way. But I'm not cosigning the bullshit or your feelings any longer."

"Let's get out of here where we aren't wanted. I'll take you home," I told her. That was the only thing I could think to say to stop her from going off on my ass.

"Naw, I need some space from you. I'll take a fuckin' Uber," she snapped and walked away from me.

Robin was like a sister to me. We'd never been this mad with each other before. It hurt me to my soul to watch her walk away. It wasn't like I could've made her stay. It was in my best interest to give her some space and when she was ready to talk, she'd come back to me. What I didn't understand was how I could be that way with Robin but couldn't be that way with Scorpio. Had I not gone after him trying to get him to talk to me, I wouldn't have been standing in the hospital right now.

"What are you still doing here?" Twist reappeared. From the looks of things, he was ready to chew into my ass some more.

"I understand you blaming me for this. I blame myself too. However, you're not going to make me leave. He's still my man and I'm still in love with him. Until he tells me that he doesn't want me here, then my black ass will be parked in one of these seats, ready to see him and help him heal." It was sad that it took for something this horrible to happen for me to realize just how much I really loved him.

"Girl bye! My boy going to laugh your ass right out of this hospital. That's if his mother doesn't get to you first," he told me.

The mention of his mother made me overly nervous. He'd never mentioned his mother to me, and we certainly never mentioned me meeting her. That was cool. I'm sure it was because we hadn't been together that long, and he wanted to make sure I was the one. Meeting someone's parents is a big step. Especially, when it came to their mother.

Twist went to sit over in a corner as far away from me as he could. The longer we sat there waiting to hear something, the more scared I became. My stomach was churning with worry. We'd sat there so long that morning had arrived, so I decided to go down to the cafeteria and try to grab something to eat. Maybe the food would help ease some of my anxiety.

"Hey ma. You mighty fine," a man came strolling towards me. He called himself giving me a compliment. There was no way the way that I looked was appealing so I didn't acknowledge him. "You don't hear me talking to you? I said you were fine," he repeated.

The man was ugly as fuck. It's crazy how the ugliest people be the quickest ones to try to talk to you. I looked at him and immediately thought, *if shit at the bottom of my shoe was a person.* That's how ugly he was.

Facing him, I started moving my hands like I was using sign language. The expression on his face was one to die for.

"Oh, you deaf? It's okay, I don't discriminate. You so fine, you can still get it," he told me. I almost wanted to throw up in my mouth. "It's a good thing you can't talk, I won't have to deal with you talking back. You got a phone?" He started chuckling.

He had to be kiddin' me. Why wouldn't he just go away? It was actually sad that he was still trying to holler at me.

"Tell me your name, boo." I moved my fingers like they were gang signs. That still didn't make him go away. "Damn, I bet those fingers sexy as hell during sex. You become a crip then, huh?" He laughed even harder. I must've missed the joke. I didn't see what was funny. "You get what I said? You must be a crip. Like cripple, abbreviated. I crack myself up." He continued to laugh. He laughed so hard that tears started coming from his eyes. Still, I saw nothing funny. Hoping to get him out of my face, I moved my fingers faster, making any sign I could come up with. "Damn, you ain't gotta cuss me out, I'm just trying to get to know you," he remarked. I raised a brow wondering how he got me cussing him out from me moving my fingers fast. Maybe he knew something that I didn't.

That was it for me. There was no reason for me to stand there and entertain him any longer. It was clear that he didn't understand when somebody didn't want to be bothered with him. That was a shame. I could only imagine the number of times his dumb ass was probably told off by a woman.

Instead of giving him anymore of my energy, I left from where he was and headed to grab a sandwich and some chips. After picking up a bottled water, I went up to the cashier to make my purchase.

"You found everything you needed?" the cashier asked.

"Yeah. This should do it," I replied.

"You should've tried our special. We have salmon with rice pilaf, and you get two sides and a desert for $8.99," she informed me.

"I'm good. I'm trying to watch my figure," I cracked. "It does sound good, have you tried it?"

"Yeah. I'm not really a fish eater so for me to clean my plate, that says a lot," she responded.

"Dang. It's tempting, but I really am trying to watch my weight," I told her.

"Yeah, your fat ass needs to. You stood over there acting like you were too good to talk to me but you smiling and talking all in her damn face. Oh, I get it now. You eat pussy. You could've just said that shit from the jump instead of playing all these damn games. Thirsty tri-"

Wham...

He never had the chance to finish his statement. Twist came up from behind and hit him across the head with one of the cafeteria trays. My mouth dropped. He was the last person I would expect to defend me.

"Come on. Scorpio's mother would like to speak to you. Keeping her waiting would not be a good look," he warned me.

Once I'd paid for my food, I followed Twist to where Scorpio's mother was.

"Thank you," I sincerely thanked him. He didn't know how much I appreciated him for having my back the way that he did. Scorpio would've been happy to see that.

"For what?" he bluntly asked.

"Helping me. That whole situation could've gone left if you didn't show up when you did," I commented.

"I didn't do it for you. I did it for Scorpio." It bruised my ego to hear that. I didn't understand why he hated me so much.

"Why don't you like me?" I curiously questioned him.

"To keep it a buck with you, Scorpio is more than my friend. I don't know if he told you or not, we are brothers.

If something happens to him, it happens to me. What you did tonight could've gotten us all killed. He's fighting for his life because you didn't listen. That hardheaded shit not gon' cut it. If he wants to be with you after this, I'd be surprised. You better hope he pulls through." He rambled on without really telling me what the real issue was. He said it was about what happened tonight. It seemed to me that maybe I was missing something. I couldn't worry about it. Scorpio was my main concern. If Twist didn't like me, so what? He wasn't the first person that didn't fuck with me and I'm sure he wouldn't be the last. He could dislike me all he wanted. His ass was still going to respect me.

"What about Robin?"

"What about her?"

"Are you going to be able to forgive her? I messed up, not her."

"She was with you. That makes her as guilty as you are."

"You're wrong."

"Don't tell me what I am. What happens between Robin and I is our business. Worry about my brother and if he stays alive. He dies, you goin' with him," he threatened.

"Well damn, thank you anyways." In my opinion, saying that to him showed that I was the bigger person. It worried me that he thought it was okay to threaten me. As soon as Scorpio was okay, I was going to make sure he knew about it. I bet he'd make it where Twist's ass won't threaten no damn body else.

By the time we made it back to where Scorpio's mother was, Twist's whole vibe had changed. He was like a completely different person.

"Hey Momma Trina, this is Mignon, Scorpio's girlfriend," he introduced me.

"Oh, I see. So, you're the BITCH that got my son shot," she spat. My eyes grew big and wide.

"Excuse me?"

"You heard what I said. Twist told me everything. Your stupidity is what got my son shot. I'll tell you what... Since I'm sure you're like the other hussies that have tried to be with him, I'm going to make you an offer you can't refuse," she stated.

"Are you trying to offer me money? Do you think you can buy me off so that I will stay away from your son?"

"Why not? You look like you could use the money."

"I'm trying my best to be real respectful right now. You're pushing me. If I were you, I'd find somebody else to play with."

"You have one time to disrespect me and I can guarantee you that I won't have to give you a dime. The minute my son finds out the way you came at me, you won't ever have to worry about hearing from him again."

"Is that what you think?"

"Think! No honey, that's what I know," she assured me.

"Why'd you come get me for this? If I wanted to argue with someone, I could've found some random bitch in the cafeteria to argue with. I don't have time for this. I'm going over here to wait for my man to get out of surgery."

"He won't be your man for much longer, honey," his mother taunted.

"Bitch, kiss my ass!" I spat before walking away.

Don't think I'm crazy. There was nothing wrong with the way I handled her. I approached her on my nice, good girl shit. She came at me wrong for no reason. I understood she was upset about what happened with Scorpio, she had every right to be. Hell, I was upset too. I loved him just as much as she did and didn't want anything to happen to him. Not to mention, I've been blaming myself since everything happened. Then it dawned on me that Robin was right.

The person that came flying out of nowhere shooting at him had it out for Scorpio. Nobody else ended up being shot. Why was that? It doesn't take a rocket scientist to realize that they were out to get him. Robin was right when she said if they wanted to get him, whether it was that night or during a different time, they were going to make it happen. Why should I continue to beat myself up over something I had no control over? Even worse, why should I allow someone else to beat me up?

My love for Scorpio was not going to change. Yeah, I had to put his mother in her place. He should be able to understand that. It doesn't matter who you are, there isn't a single person on earth better than the next. No matter what place she held in his life, she was going to have to learn to respect me because I planned to be around for the rest of his life. Either she was going to be my friend, or she was going to be my enemy. The choice was hers.

Chapter Thirty:

Javi

(One Week Later...)

Keeping my ear to the streets, I was disappointed to learn that Scorpio didn't die. I should've known that if I wanted the shit done right, I should've done it myself. Not only did I have to kill Scorpio for going after Mignon, I had to kill Twist for fuckin' with Shawnte behind my back. He even got the bitch pregnant.

Today, I had a meeting with the plug. He supplied Scorpio with all of his product. Since he was out of commission right now, someone needed to pick up the slack. I heard Twist wasn't doing much of shit because he was too busy guarding Scorpio. That was fine by me.

Going into the kitchen, I pulled the two bags of ice out of there that I purchased last night. Taking a knife, I cut a hole in them and took them into the guest bedroom. Opening the three bins I had in there, I checked to see which one I wanted to move out when I left the apartment. It seemed that the bin in the middle would be the easiest for me to move, so I poured a bag of ice each into the other two bins before placing the lids back on them.

The day that Shawnte disclosed to me that her son wasn't really mine, I blacked out. I banged her head against the floor so much that I never realized she'd stopped fighting me. By the time that I did, it was too late. I'd killed her. Knowing I couldn't call the police or take her out the apartment without any of the nosey ass neighbors figuring out what was going on, I used a saw and cut her body up. I divided her body parts into five different bins and decided it would be best for me to take the parts to different states to bury them.

Shawnte's mother called a few times looking for her so I told her that she ran off with some man she met. Since I convinced her mother that she had a history of doing this, her mother didn't push the issue. She asked me if I wanted to come see my son, I told her that I would make time to visit him when I wasn't busy working. She didn't know I didn't have a job, so that was a good cover for me. There was no way I could tell her that I knew Javi Jr. wasn't mine. That would cause her to worry and put more thought into where Shawnte could be. That was something I didn't need. Not right now.

Today, I was going to dispose of the third bin. I'd driven the first one to Houston and the second one to Little Rock. I left both her phone and my phone at the apartment. That way nobody would be able to ping my locations. If I needed to talk to someone, I'd borrow a phone from someone else.

Knock... Knock...

"Who the fuck could that be?" I asked myself before heading towards the front door. We never had visitors and I wasn't expecting anyone so there was no reason for anybody to be knocking on the door. "Who is it?" I yelled once I was close enough to the door.

"Dino." Quickly, I snatched the door open and told him to come inside.

"What the fuck are you doing here?" I asked.

"I need that money you promised me for handling Scorpio. I need to get out of town," he advised me.

"You didn't do what I was paying you to do. I said kill him. That nigga laid up in the hospital and they are expecting a full recovery from what I heard."

"Fuck all that. Twist is beating the streets trying to find the person responsible for this shit. I'm not bout to go down for this."

"And I'm not paying for a job that wasn't done. You better take that shit up with some damn body else."

"So, you telling me I risked my life for nothing?"

"If the light company didn't turn your lights on and sent you a bill, you gonna pay the shit? I ain't thank so. Get the fuck outta here thinking I'm bout to pay you when you ain't did shit," I barked.

"Aight. You ain't heard the last from me," he warned. That shit meant nothing. He couldn't kill Scorpio so there was no way he'd kill me. Nigga better get out my face before I put a bug in Twist's ear and lead him straight to his ass.

Dino stormed out of my apartment. I could tell he was going to be a problem. I made a mental note to follow his ass for a while because something about him didn't sit well with me.

Slamming the door and locking it behind him, I decided to shoot Mignon a text to see if she'd give me some information on how Scorpio was doing. With any luck, there would be a change in his health, and he took a turn for the worse.

Me: Hey Mignon! I no I'm da last person u wont to here 4rom. I wonted to check on u an Scorpio.

After waiting thirty minutes without a reply, I sent her another text. She knew I hated being ignored. It seemed like she was doing the shit to get under my skin.

Me: Let me no u good. Damn!

Mignon: NOT TUH DAE! I'm not about to deal with you. Me and Scorpio are just fine. Goodbye!

She was rude as fuck! All I wanted to do was find out if she was okay or not. She didn't have to come at me the way that she did.

Me: Dats y I hate u damn GEMI-FUKIN-NIS! Fuck u Mignon.

Mignon: Naw. I'm good. Scorpio fucks me well. It's the best I ever had. Keep that shriveled up dick over ←↑→↓ there. Lol

It was in my best interest not to respond. She wanted me to pop off. That would've been another excuse for her to say we wouldn't work. It was all good. Mignon was going to be taught all over again, what happens when you cross me.

Beep... Beep... Beep... Beep...

My alarm started going off. It was alerting me that it was time for me to make my drive. The third bin that contained parts of Shawnte's body was being transported to Atlanta. Fuckin' with Dino and Mignon, I'd almost gotten off schedule.

Dragging the bin to the front door, I went back to the guest bedroom and stacked the remaining two bins inside the closet. The ice was used to keep her bod from smelling. If everything worked out in my favor, I would've fully deposited her remains by the end of the week. I was tactful by how I did things because if people kept seeing me leaving with bins, that would be another reason for them to be suspicious. I tried my best to make everything seem as normal as possible.

Locking up, I loaded Shawnte up in her shotgun ass car and got inside. Silently saying a prayer, I struggled for ten minutes to crank the car. Once it started, I was on my way. Shawnte's lower body was on their way to their new home in Atlanta. It was sad that she had to go out like that. She was a beautiful woman. I once believed that she was beautiful inside and out. The more time I spent with her, the more I realized that it was all just a front. She was nothing but a mistake. My prayer was that her being a mistake was not enough to land me back behind bars.

Chapter Thirty-One:

Mignon

When the doctor came out and told us that Scorpio was hit three times, I could've died. My anxiety level quickly shot through the rough. It bothered me that they had to put him in a coma to help ease some of the pain that he was in. They also thought that it would help him to start healing faster. *The less movement he made, the better his chances were for a speedy recovery.* That's what I kept telling myself. The doctor seemed to think that moving around would help him heal faster and better.

Twist and I both stayed at the hospital. There was no way we were going to leave him alone. We both were worried that someone would come back and try to finish the job. His dumb ass mother would pop in and out. I'm sure she was more concerned with how she was going to continue to live the lifestyle she lived with him not being around. That was probably wrong for me to think that way, but so what? The whole time we'd been together, I'd never seen him talk to her or go visit her. Hell, I honestly thought his parents were dead.

"Anything change?" Twist asked, stomping into the room like he had a problem. His phone was going off constantly. He had gotten into it with Robin and broke up with her so who the hell was he talking to.

"He's still the same," I sassed.

"What's with the attitude?"

"You think I wanted him here. I'm sick of being blamed for what happened," I snapped.

"Mignon, I'm not doing this shit with you. I'm not about to argue with you while my homeboy sitting there fighting for his life."

"You don't want to argue with me, huh? I'm sure that's because someone else is harboring your time."

"Are we fuckin'?"

"No. Why would you ask me something like that?"

"You acting like we are. We are here for one reason and that reason is laying in that bed, unresponsive. What I do has nothing to do with you," he chided.

"Fine. Bet you won't be saying that when I tell Robin," I threatened.

"Tell Robin, she not my momma," he returned.

Twist had found a way to get under my skin. That wasn't a good thing at all. If we were both going to be in Scorpio's life, we had to find a way to get along. That wasn't happening and it was sad. Scorpio would have a fit if he saw us bickering the way that we were. Thinking about it did something to me. It had to stop.

"Twist, before tonight, we had a good relationship. I understand you're upset with me. I would be too. I'm not saying you don't have a right to be mad. At least let's be cordial until Scorpio is better. He needs both of us."

"He don't need you. He has me. When he wakes up and thinks about how your actions led to this, I can assure you that you won't be around too much longer. So, enjoy the time you have with him now; it'll be over soon," he spoke and left out the room.

"Baby, I just don't know. I'm trying to be here for you, but these people are pushing me. It's been a tough week. You don't know all the things I've had to endure since you've been like this. Please come back to me. You said you'd be there for me and that you'd always protect me. I know I was wrong for not listening to you. I swear the only thing on my mind that night was making things better with us. I love you baby. I want to move in with you. I want for us to get married one day and I have all your babies. That can't happen as long as you're like this. Please baby. Come back to me so we can build a future together." That needed to be said. It was the way I truly felt.

BEEEEEEPPPPPPP....

A loud beeping sound could be heard throughout the room. Suddenly, Scorpio's eyes popped open.

"What the fuck is going on? What did you do to him?" Twist ran in, ready to blame me for doing something else to Scorpio. I was over it.

"He woke up," was the only thing I could say to Twist as I tried to gather myself and make sure it wasn't a dream.

Chapter Thirty-Two:

Scorpio

My soul left my body. That was the wakeup call I needed to know it was time for me to walk away from this street shit. The one thing I could say about this whole experience, I knew who was down for me. Although I'd been out of it, I could hear everyone that came and went from the doctors, nurses, my crew, my righthand man, and my crazy ass mother. Out of all the people who came, Mignon was the one that I wanted by my side more than anything.

Opening my eyes for the first time in what seemed like forever, they fluttered at the light shining in through the window. Mignon always made it a point to open the damn blinds because she claimed it allowed God's grace to shine down on me or something like that. It was cute when she would come in and pray for me. If you would've heard some of the shit she talked about you would laugh your ass off.

BEEEEEEPPPPPPP....

One of the machines made a loud beeping sound. I'm not sure which one it was, but it had gotten on my nerves that quick. It wasn't the beeping sound that bothered me, it was how loud it was.

Twist busted inside the room hollering, "What the fuck is going on? What did you do to him?" He was ready to blame Mignon if anything was wrong with me. That's why Twist was my nigga. He'd be ready to put anybody down that he felt caused me any harm or that was a threat to me.

"He woke up," Mignon stated. The tone in her voice showed that she was surprised.

Being who I was, I wish I could've told Mignon everything was going to be okay. I hated that she and Twist had to sit around the hospital the way that they did, worried about what was going to happen with me. They should've known I was going to come out on top because I was never the type of man that gave up on anything. Mignon should've known that by how persistent I was to get her.

"Baby, I'm here. Don't try to move. Let them check you out first." Mignon jumped up from her chair and sprinted towards the door. She came back with five different people that worked in the hospital. Twist wasn't far behind. If I knew him, his ass had been sleeping in a chair outside my room making sure nobody could come in and fuck with me while I wasn't able to protect myself.

"Water..." I requested. My mouth was dryer than Aniya's stale ass pussy.

"Hol' on, baby. Let them check you out first to make sure you're good."

Those damn folks poked and touched me so much, you would've thought I was famous.

"You are truly a blessed man, Mr. Dewitt. I'm Dr. Frazier. I've been tending to you since you were admitted. Your body underwent a lot of trauma. Honestly, it had me worried."

"I don't know why. My son's a fighter. I knew he would be ever since he was in my womb. That lil' nigga used to kick me so hard that I peed on myself at least twice a day," my mother announced. All I could do was drop my head. *At what age did your mother stop embarrassing you?* "How's he doing, doc?"

"From the looks of things, he's doing very well. He's going to be back on his feet in no time."

"Can I get that water now?" I asked again. I didn't do that asking twice shit, so they'd better get to it before I turned the damn hospital upside down.

"Is it safe for him to have?" Mignon asked the doctor.

"Yes. Give him a little. Not too much. I want to send him for a few tests. If everything checks out okay, he'll be ready to go home in a few days," the doctor explained.

"A few days? I'm ready to go now. I feel fine hell. Twist, grab my shit so we can bounce."

"Baby, stop. Let the doctors take care of you. You need to make sure you're perfectly fine to leave before you jump up and go."

"You are not my mother, Mignon. Give me the damn water and my clothes so I can go."

"Don't talk to me like that, Scorpio." Mignon was already starting to get on my nerves. She tried to put the cup of water up to my mouth, but I snatched it out of her hand.

"I can do it myself," I grunted. She stood back and watched. My hand was shaking uncontrollably. I didn't understand what was going on with me. "What the fuck!" I roared. "Why is my shit shaking like this?"

"You were in a coma for over a week. It's going to take your body getting used to you doing certain things again."

"You mean to tell me my dick not going to work either? What the fuck kinda shit is that? Mignon come sit on this big mufucka and see if I still got it," I demanded. Everyone in the room stared at me like I'd lost my damn mind. I wasn't joking though. I was getting ready to pull up my gown until she stopped me.

"Stop acting like that. I understand that you're upset about what happened, but you have to listen to the doctor," Mignon fussed.

"Didn't I just tell you that you weren't my mother?" I grunted, throwing the cup of water up against the wall.

"You need to leave, Mignon. Nobody wants you here," my mother chimed in.

"I'm not leaving. I deserve to be here as much as you and Twist do. I love him too," Mignon asserted.

"Love isn't always enough. You see what your love did? It caused him to get shot up," my mother muttered.

"I'm sorry, Scorpio. You may dislike me after this, but enough is enough. I refuse to let anyone disrespect me,"

Mignon said before focusing her attention on my mother. "You got me fucked up. I don't give a damn that he can see me going off on you. You will not keep coming at me like I'm not shit. I love the fuck out of your son, but I love myself more. You are going to respect me one way or another. Keep on fuckin' with me and see won't I help you meet Jesus a little faster. You're too damn old to be in your son's business. He obviously loves me. If he didn't, I wouldn't be here. If you don't like that than so fuckin' what. You aren't fuckin', feedin', or financin' either one of us. And that's on PERIOD POOH!"

"Well, I never..."

"You may have never, but your ass is gonna... GONNA FUCKIN' RESPECT ME OR CATCH THESE MUTHAFUCKIN' HANDS!" Mignon spat. At that point, my mother shut up. I'm sure she was waiting on me to interject, but there was no point in me doing so. Right was right and wrong was wrong. In this instance, my mother was definitely wrong.

"You going to let her talk to me like that? I'm your mother."

"You were wrong, and you know how I feel about disrespect. Mignon didn't do anything to you."

"She got you shot."

"I got myself shot. She had nothing to do with that."

"Bullshit if she didn't. Had she took her naggin' ass on like you asked her to, we wouldn't have still been there where somebody had the chance to get at you," Twist roared.

"I got you, bro. Trust me, I had that same thought. At the same time, whomever got me had to be plotting and waiting for us. It was going to happen at some point or another," I admitted. Every street nigga knew that there was going to be competition. There was going to be someone gunning to take you down so they could take your place. I was lucky to get away with nobody coming for me for as long as I'd been in the game. Truth be told, if I really thought about it, I was sure I could pinpoint who was behind the shit.

"Wow. You really do love her. My bad, bro," Twist apologized. "I'm sorry, Mignon. I felt some type of way about my nigga being shot. I shouldn't have blamed you. It seemed like the right thing to do at the time."

"I understand. I accept your apology as long as you try to make things right with my girl. She loves you." Twist started laughing. "What's funny?"

"Robin came over that same night and we made up. I've been punishing that pussy on a regular."

"I believe that's our cue to leave," Dr. Frazier said.

"Do I have to leave? This has been the most entertainment I've had in weeks," one of the nurses joked. Everyone in the room laughed. Dr. Frazier shook his head and left the rom. "Y'all stay put. I have another eleven hours on my shift. I'll be back to enjoy the show," she teased. At least I thought she was joking.

With everyone out the room, my mother kept her eyes trained on Mignon. She was used to getting her way. Women bowed down to her thinking it would make me keep them around. That didn't work with me. It was a sign of weakness. I needed someone who could be strong and that was definitely Mignon. My mother had no choice but to deal with it. I was grown and it was time she allowed me to live my life with the person I chose to live it with.

Chapter Thirty-Three:

Javi

Dumping Shawnte's body turned out to be easier than I expected. Her mother still called to see if I'd heard from her and I told her no. Since I told her that Shawnte left me, it didn't dawn on me that I needed to get rid of her phone. If her mother went to the police, the first thing they'd do was ping her phone back to our apartment.

Knock... Knock...

"Damn. Here we go with this shit again," I said to myself. I took my time getting to the door. As I walked, I thought about the last unexpected visitor that I had. Dino's ass was going to have to go. He'd called my phone relentlessly, trying to get money out of me. That wasn't going to happen because he didn't do what I was going to pay him to do.

"Where's my daughter?" The moment I opened the door, Shawnte's mother came walking in. She didn't even give me the chance to invite her in. She had Javi Jr. right along with her.

"I told you she left me. Why you keep trying to find her like y'all had a good relationship anyway?" That was my way of trying to throw her off and hopefully, make her leave.

"What are you talking about? Shawnte and I had a great relationship. We've only been having a problem lately because I kept telling her to leave your good for nothing ass."

"I don't have time for this shit. Leave Brenda. Go away just like Shawnte did. I got other shit to handle."

"You told me that you loved my daughter. Why'd you lie?"

"Lie? I don't have to lie to you about anything. I know where my heart is. Your daughter doesn't love me the way she claims. She was ready to leave with the next nigga she thought would give her the life she wanted. She was all about money and when I couldn't give her the money and life she wanted, she ran to the next man," I told her mother. Although that may have seemed mean, we both knew how her daughter really was. At least, I thought she knew.

"Don't talk about my daughter like she's some type of hoe or something."

"I'm not talking about her. I'm telling you how she is and you and I both know that's the truth. I don't have to make her seem like something she really is."

"Fuck you, Javi. My daughter is a good woman. She loves you." I'm not sure if she was trying to convince me or herself. Either way, I wasn't convinced.

"Naw. I fucked your daughter. Her pussy was terrible, and I can imagine she got it honestly. Find somebody else to fuck," I spat. "And stop telling me that she loves me. She loves me enough to make me raise a child that isn't mine?" Brenda's mouth dropped open when I said that. Shawnte never had the chance to tell her that I knew the truth because I killed her before she got the chance to.

Brenda tried to go back and forth with me for the next thirty minutes. She was really fussing with herself because I wasn't responding. Once I'd gotten rid of her, I waited for night to fall. Twist and Scorpio had betrayed me after I damn near killed myself working for them and making sure they ate. They had to die! I was determined to make that happen soon and very soon.

Chapter Thirty-Four:

Mignon

(One Month Later...)

"Are you okay, baby?" I asked Scorpio, who had been moving around as if nothing had happened to him. Every time I reminded him that he had been shot and had to have major surgery, that fool looked at me like he wanted to kill me. That's why I don't too much say anything else about it.

"I'm cool. Stop asking me that," he grunted.

"Damn. All I did was ask a question. I don't need you jumping down my throat," I refuted.

"I keep telling your ass that I'm good. Stop asking me the same shit over and over again. My answer isn't going to change," he fussed.

Scorpio had pissed me off just that fast. It didn't make sense that he acted that way towards me. It had me wondering if he was upset with me about the shooting incident and didn't want to tell me.

"I'm sorry, ma." He came towards me and wrapped his arms around me.

"Why are you snapping on me like that?"

"Cuz you won't give a nigga no pussy. It's been weeks." He was dead ass serious. Scorpio looked like he was ready to shoot some shit up for some pussy. I couldn't help it. I had to laugh at his ass. "What the fuck is so funny?" he snarled.

"I'm sorry, baby. You are being so dramatic right now." Scorpio began kissing me on the neck. We both knew what he was doing. We'd had plenty of conversations where I told him that kissing on my neck did something to me. That moment proved to be correct because my panties were soaked.

"Take that shit off," he ordered. I did exactly what he said. He went and laid in the bed on his back. I was able to see the marks from where he'd been shot and immediately, I was scared. "You're not going to hurt me," he told me.

Nothing he said was going to change how I was feeling. He hadn't had sex in a while, so he was going to try to go all out. That made me think he was going to hurt himself. I had to make the executive decision to give him head. Sucking his dick to the point that he nutted should've been enough to tire him out and make him not want pussy. That's what I kept thinking.

From the end of the bed, I was on my knees crawling towards him. He had a devilish grin on his face. He was happy as hell. Stopping at his waist, I opened my mouth as wide as I could before taking as much of his dick inside of it as I could.

"Sssss..." he hissed right as I began sucking it. I started going slow so that he'd be able to enjoy it more. After a while, he began thrusting up in my mouth. I wanted to pull back because he was going deep as hell. Remember, I'd only been with Javi, so I wasn't a pro at the shit.

"Chill out, baby. I'm trying," I pulled back and said.

"I'm trying to teach you how I like it. You might as well start getting used to it since I'm the last man you gonna be with," he commented.

"Whatever." I rolled my eyes before I commenced to suckin' his dick. As bad as I wanted to feel him inside of me, I'd have to settle for giving him head until I heard from the doctor that he could resume normal activity.

As before, Scorpio picked up the pace and began fuckin' my mouth. His dick was going deeper down my throat than I'd previously allowed it to go. This caused me to gag.

"That's right, take all this dick, baby."

Fuck it, I thought. Removing my mouth, I spit on my hand and began massaging it on his dick and balls. As I stroked his dick, I used my mouth to give his balls attention. Scorpio began moaning. His thrusts never stopped. My mouth made its way back up to his dick. I sucked it as if my life depended on it. I went from suckin' to slurpin', to lickin', and then repeat before moving my mouth up and focusing solely on the tip of his dick.

"Fuck girl! You bout to make me cum. Come get on this dick!" he demanded, I acted as if I didn't hear him. "Come ride it, baby," he repeated. Again, I ignored him.

Swiftly, he placed his hands under my arms and pulled me up. Without hesitation, he slammed me down on his dick. I wanted to die. I hadn't gotten used to his size and we had only had sex one time before.

"I'm not trying to hurt you," he said. What should've been moans coming from me was more of me crying from the pain.

"I know," I told him. A few moments of me sitting there, I began grinding on his dick and trying to get used to it being inside of me.

"See, had you gave me the pussy earlier, you wouldn't be going through this shit right now." His ass had the nerve to display this big cheesy ass grin. I wanted to mule kick his mufuckin' ass.

"Shut up," I spat before playfully rolling my eyes.

Since he wanted to talk shit, I picked up my pace with riding him. He gripped my waist and tried to slow me down. Nothing he did worked. It was clear that he was hurting but I couldn't tap out. I wouldn't tap out. He was delivering thrusts so deep that I felt like he was rearranging my insides. It hurt but felt so good at the same time. I wanted more. I couldn't get enough of Scorpio.

"You're about to make me cum," I announced.

"Let that shit out, baby. Cream all over your dick," he ordered. As soon as the words left his mouth, my body was jerking as I came all over his dick. My pussy was doing Kegels on his dick as I continued to cum. It wasn't long before he was cumin' right behind me.

Having Scorpio inside of me was the best feeling in the world. As bad as he wanted me, I wanted him too. This gave me further confirmation that I really wanted to be with him and only him. I was also scared. Whomever shot at Scorpio was clearly trying to kill him. Since they didn't kill him the first time, I wondered if they were going to come back and try it again and if they'd come after me if they couldn't get to him. It was a lot to think about, but I couldn't erase those thoughts. That was never going to happen until the person that did this to Scorpio was forced to be punished for his acts.

Chapter Thirty-Five:

Scorpio

Mignon wasn't fooling me, and I knew I wasn't fooling her. Yet, she was taking this dick like a champ. It hurt like hell for me to be fuckin' her the way that I was, but I knew that if I would've given her some mediocre dick, she would've known that my body was in excruciating pain and probably wouldn't give up the pussy again no time soon. I couldn't have that.

"Come on, baby," she told me as we laid there holding each other. She hopped out the bed and pranced towards the bathroom.

"Where we going?" I questioned.

"I'm about to run you some water to soak in. You need it after that." She giggled with her head hanging out of the bathroom door, causing me to laugh. "You laughin' because you know I'm telling the truth. How you gonna be hurting and still want the pussy?"

"How your pussy so mufuckin' good? Baby, somebody could shoot me while I was all inside of you and I bet you I'd still be strokin' like ain't shit happen. That pussy addictive as fuck," I admitted to her. That was no lie.

Mignon was walking around with a gold mine between her legs. It was a shame I had to wait this fuckin' long to get it.

"I'm not bout to play with you. Get up and start making your way towards the bathroom," she instructed. Due to still recovering, I was moving a little slower than normal. That's why I hadn't gone back to being heavy in the streets yet. That time was coming very soon. If I didn't do anything else, I was going to get to the bottom of who shot me.

When I stepped inside the bathroom, I was intrigued to see that Mignon had candles lit around a bubble bath.

"What's all this? This some shit for a female," I barked.

"Shut up, crazy. I'm doing something to show my appreciation for my man."

"Oh, now I'm your man?" I cheesed hard as hell.

"No," she replied. My eyebrows flew up. "You're my future. My world. My protector. My everything." She placed soft gentle kisses around my face. Instantly, my dick bricked up again.

"What's with the mushy shit?" I joked.

"Oh, so me showing you how I feel about you is mushy?" She frowned up.

"That's not what I'm saying at all, ma. Can I show you something though?" I asked, licking my lips.

"No. Unh unh. Get in the tub, Scorpio," she demanded. She stood there pouting with her arms crossed over her chest. That didn't bother me one bit. It only added to the intensity I had inside of me to want to drop this dick off inside of her.

With one swift motion, I spun her around and bent her over the tub.

"Ba-. Oh, my gawwwddd..." she exclaimed as soon as I entered her. She was soaking wet.

"This my pussy, ma."

"Yes, baby. It's yours."

"I'm not asking you. I'm telling you," I grunted as I pumped deep inside of her. She held on to the tub as best she could. When she couldn't maintain her balance, she started dropping until she was on her knees. Every time she dropped, I dropped down with her. We were both on our knees, with me still beating her pussy up.

"Fuck Scorpio. Keep fuckin' me, baby. Shiittttt!!! I love your dick, baby," she exhaled. That was like music to my ears. Despite the pain I was feeling, I didn't miss a beat with her. I gave Mignon as much pleasure as I possibly could. My goal was to make it where she'd never think of another man again. Especially, not Javi's sorry ass.

Bam... Bam...

"Baby, someone is beating on the door," Mignon stated. I heard the shit and I didn't care. I kept delivering mind blowing strokes to her. She tried to stand up but each time she tried, I pumped harder. After three pumps, she gave up. Her words became slurred and her moans became increasingly loud. "Shit, why you doing this to me?"

"Doing what?"

"Why... are... you... fuckin'... me... so... good...?" She stuttered. "I'm cumin'," she announced.

"Me too, baby," I replied as we reached our climax together. Even though she never confirmed anything, I knew her ass had to have been pregnant from the first time we were together. If she wasn't, she surely had to be this time.

Bam... Bam...

"Who the fuck is that?" I muttered pissed off that all I wanted to do was enjoy being with my girl and couldn't even do that.

"You want me to get it?" Mignon asked.

"Really? I'm not, Javi. I'll never put you in a situation where you could get hurt," I told her.

"We don't even know who it is," she stated.

"That's an even bigger reason for you to not go to the door. Whomever it is has to be out of their damn mind for beating on my fuckin' door. I didn't ask for no damn company," I advised her.

Ring... Ring...

My phone rang and I still didn't budge. My dick was still resting inside of Mignon.

"Sit down and let me grab your phone," she told me. It took me a while, but I managed to sit on the side of the tub. My eyes stayed on Mignon as she left out of the bathroom. She came back in smiling, handing me my phone. I attempted to pull her down in my lap, but she pulled back.

Ring... Ring...

"It's Twist. Get that and let me go get your medicine. I know your ass is hurting." She winked at me and sashayed away. "Oh, and tell Twist you won't be coming out to play today," she stopped in the doorway and said.

"I hear you, ma," I replied before answering the phone. "This better be important. I'm trying to make up for lost time over here."

"Mannnn, open the door. This shit hella important," he quipped. That caused me to jump up off the shower and head inside the room. I threw on a pair of basketball shorts and went towards the front door.

"Where are you going?" Mignon came running behind me.

"Twist at the door. Something's up," I told her.

Twist was profusely sweating when I opened the door. He pushed past me and grabbed ahold of Mignon. Pushing her up against the wall, I ran towards him and punched that nigga in the back of the head.

"Nigga, what the fuck up with you?" I asked.

"Ask that bitch what's up with her. Ask her why the fuck Javi was the reason someone tried to kill you." When he said that, I stood there like the life had been sucked out of me. Surely, I didn't hear him correctly.

"What is he talking about?" I turned and asked Mignon. She stood there shaking in fear. "Don't get quiet now. Say something," I growled.

"I don't know. I don't have anything to do with this. I would never do anything to hurt you. You've got to believe me," she pleaded with me.

"How can I believe you? Before you came in my life, shit was good. I'd never been shot at or shot period. Niggas knew not to try me. Suddenly, you pop up and a nigga ends up fighting for his life. At the hands of the nigga that you claim fucked you over," I fussed.

"I knew she was bad news. We need to get rid of her," Twist suggested. He threw his hands up in the air and began pacing.

It was killing me to second guess Mignon. I loved shorty. She gave me feelings no other woman on this earth ever had. If it was possible to make all this shit go away so we could be happy, I'd do it. Twist was my best friend and brother. He'd never led me astray. Mignon was my woman and she had my heart. At the same time, the shit seemed suspect. Twist was right about one thing. It wasn't until she came into my life that shit start going wrong.

"Scorpio, when you came to me about giving you a chance, I constantly pushed you away. I told you I didn't want anything to do with you. I told you to stay away from me. Why the hell would I do all of that if I wanted to set you up? If I wanted to get you killed all I had to do was go for your advances from the jump and have you meet me somewhere for Javi to get you. I'm not that type of person and you know that. You know me," she asserted. That's when I fucked up.

Gazing into her eyes, I realized I was wrong. There was no way she could've set me up the way that Twist was saying. Mignon loved me.

"She's not lying," I tried to convince him.

"What? Are you out of your mind? She's behind this shit," he chided. There was no changing his mind.

"What makes you so certain? How do you even know Javi was behind this?"

"Come with me," he said. Twist pushed past a tearful Mignon. I was right behind him. We went outside and over to his car. He popped the trunk and inside was this neighborhood nigga named Dino. He was known around the way for being a crackhead.

"Sit him up," I demanded. I needed to see something. As soon as he removed the covering from over his eyes and the tape from around his mouth, I was able to see that Dino was indeed the same person that shot at me. "Speak," I told him.

"Javi made me do it. He said he'd pay me to kill you. He was mad because you stole his girl from you, and you took his job away. You were keeping him from eating."

"You thought killing me was going to help him get her back or eat? Nobody respects him now nor will they ever respect him. Too bad for you that you risked your life for nothing," I told him.

Twist already knew what to do. He pulled out his gun that was equipped with a silencer.

"Lay down," he directed. "Say one word and I'm killing you," he told him. Dino was scared so he did exactly what

Twist said. Without warning, Twist let two shots off in Dino's head.

"Get this shit cleaned up and get rid of this car. Come back later. Javi won't live to see another day," I confirmed.

Twist hopped in the car and sped away. Since I could no longer blame this on Mignon, I knew I needed to talk to her about it all. That talk was going to have to wait. Javi was heavily on my mind. It was time for all of this shit to end once and for all.

Chapter Thirty-Six:

Javi

It was finally time for me to leave the apartment I once shared with Shawnte. I'd been putting it off until I heard about Dino running to rat me out to Twist on yesterday. It ended up backfiring on him because nobody had heard from his ass since. He probably thought if he told Twist the truth, they'd pay him for the information. That was dumb considering who he shot. He was doomed the minute he opened his mouth to call himself being noble.

Everything that I owed was in Shawnte's car. I'd hustled up a few dollars to get away from Mississippi. Turns out when I met with Scorpio's supplier, his ass wouldn't budge. He was loyal to Scorpio for whatever reason. Knowing that Dino told on me and I'm sure Scorpio's supplier was eventually going to tell him that I came to him trying to take his spot, there was going to be a bounty over my head; if there wasn't already.

Giving the apartment one last look over to make sure I had everything, I headed for the door. It was a bittersweet moment. Never in a million years would I have pictured my life being as fucked up as it was in that very moment.

All that thinking the grass was greener on the other side shit got to me. My greed for money and lust for other women had finally turned around to be my karma.

Whap...

(Two hours later...)

Groggily, I opened my eyes. I didn't know where I was, but I felt the blood dripping from my forehead.

"What the fuck!" I hollered when I realized I'd been tied to a chair.

"You finally decided to wake up, Sleeping Beauty?" Scorpio stood before me and teased. He and Twist were laughing hard as hell, but I hadn't found shit to be funny.

"Let me go. Why the fuck y'all got me tied to this chair?" I questioned, even though I already knew the answer.

"Why did you send somebody to kill me?" Scorpio asked.

"Send somebody to kill you? Do I look dumb to you or some shit? Why the hell would I do that?" I continued to play dumb.

"Cut the bullshit, Javi. I'm not about to go back and forth with you. We have already talked to Dino. We also found the nigga that was with him the night of the shooting. He showed us text conversations of you telling them what you want them to do to me. All of this over a bitch you claimed never made you happy!"

"She didn't have to make me happy. She was my bitch and for you to go after her was foul as fuck."

"What difference does it make? You were leaving her."

"YOU BROKE THE BRO CODE," I hollered. I considered Scorpio to be a friend. For him to go after my woman stunned me because that was never something I'd known him to do. If he hadn't done it to anyone else, why'd he do it to me?

"She told you she didn't want you. There was no changing that, no matter what you tried to do to get her to believe that you'd changed. You came after me and fucked up when you didn't leave me for dead. Now, you're going to have to pay for the shit. Before you die, know that Mignon and my seed will be well taken care of. Remember, one man's trash is another man's treasure. I'm going to treasure her for the rest of our lives. Go ahead and handle him, Twist," he demanded. Twist started moving towards me. I was scared out of my mind. He wasn't trying to torture me or give me a chance to explain my actions. That's how I knew for sure that I'd fucked up.

How could I be so damn stupid? If I wouldn't have switched up on Mignon when I started making a little money, I wouldn't be in the current situation I was in. The sad part was that there was no coming back from it. Scorpio said what he said and the look in Twist's eyes let me know that this was the end of the line for me.

"Can you do one last thing for me?" I asked.

"Nigga, this ain't death row. You may be about to be executed, but ain't no way in hell we are taking last requests," Scorpio told me. That nigga was cold as fuck. I couldn't say that I blamed him. If I were in his shoes, I'd probably react the same way.

"All I want you to do is to tell Mignon that I love her and I'm sorry. I never meant to hurt her like this. If I could take it back, I would. Tell her that my body and spirit won't be at peace until she forgives me," I admitted.

"You're going to be in hell. You don't need forgiveness," Twist stated before sending three bullets my way.

Scorpio walked up on me and stood before my slumped over body. While I was fighting to live, he decided it was best for him to taunt me. He went through his phone flipping through pictures of him and Mignon. Seeing her happy with another man was it for me. I at least took my last breath knowing that she was happy.

Epilogue:

Mignon

(Four Months Later...)

When Scorpio left the house that night, I knew he was going to make sure he ended Javi's life. Yeah, I hated Javi for what he'd done to me, but I never wanted him dead. The things that he put me through only showed me what I was worth and deserved. Scorpio did a great job of upholding my thoughts.

Scorpio came home that night and I was sitting up on the couch waiting for him. I told him how sorry I was that all of this happened and that I would walk away from him for good if that was what he wanted. He told me that he didn't want that. He apologized to me for what happened between us and because he didn't trust me the way that he should have. He vowed to me that he would never put me in a situation again where I would feel defeated or cry at the hands of him. He'd done a great job of keeping his word.

"You ready?" Scorpio asked me, stepping inside the bathroom with me. I was putting the finishing touches on my hair so that we could leave. We were going on a double date with Robin and Twist.

Twist was telling the truth when he said that he and Robin had made up. In fact, that was the only reason she was even talking to me. She let that be known when I finally got her to talk to me. I understood where she was coming from and I probably would've acted the same way with her as well. I'm glad we'd never have to find out how I'd really act. Scorpio meant the world to me and I'd get into a damn bull fight for that man. I even went as far as making things right with Twist. We were finally on good terms.

"Come on, Mignon. We have to be there soon. Are you ready?" he asked again.

"Yes, baby. I'm ready," I told Scorpio.

"You look so damn sexy, girl. I don't think we're going to make it out of the door," he told me.

"Boy, you crazy," I replied to him. "I love you," I said.

"That was random," he replied.

"There has to be a reason for me to tell you that I love you? All I want to do is let you know how much you mean to me each and every day," I informed him.

"Damn. Didn't I tell you about that mushy shit?" he joked.

"It's not being mushy. I'm just expressing my feelings for you, baby."

"I know. I wish you wouldn't have done that," he said.

"Why? What's wrong with me doing that?"

Out of nowhere, Scorpio dropped down to one knee. Tears came rushing to the forefront of my eyes. This had to be a dream.

"I had this whole dinner set up to ask you to be my wife, but this seems like the better time for me to do this," he paused. If I didn't know any better, I'd say that he had teared up.

"Are you okay?"

"Ssssshhhhhh..." *Did this nigga really just shush me*, I thought to myself. "I love you so much, Mignon. It hasn't been that long since we've gotten together, but you've changed my life for the better. I'm not sure if it's because

I've gone through more with you over these past few months than I'd ever gone through in my life or if God really sent you here just for me. Whatever the reason is, I want you to know that I wouldn't have it any other way. Love me forever, Mignon. Will you do me the honor of being my wife?"

When he dropped down to one knee, I already knew that he was going to ask me to marry him. Now that the words have actually left his mouth, I was stuck.

"Baby, will you marry me?" he asked again.

I nodded my head yes. That was the only thing I could do. It was as if I was still in complete shock.

"I don't understand gestures. Open your mouth, ma," he told me.

"Yes. Yes, I'll marry you!" I finally spoke before jumping up and down. My tears began to fall faster.

Scorpio stood from his knee and pulled me in for a big embrace. He turned my head towards his and we engaged in one of the most passionate kisses I'd ever had in my life.

"Clean your face up, we're going to have to do this all over again. Make sure you can make those tears fall again, too," he told me.

"Wait... What? Why?"

"Do you know how many people are supposed to be waiting for us? You're not about to get me cussed out. That's why I haven't shown you the ring yet. As soon as you see it, you're going to melt. I know a nigga gonna get fucked good as hell tonight. As a matter of fact, don't wear no panties, I'm taking you to the bathroom as soon as I ask you to marry me again," he said. He kissed me on the cheek and walked out the restroom.

Standing in front of the mirror, I began fixing my make up as I reflected over my life. Nobody could've told me that Javi and I wouldn't be together or that he'd be dead right now. Nobody could've even convinced me that I'd end up with Scorpio. God truly broke the mold when he made him. There was no way I could not thank God for the many blessings he bestowed upon me, with Scorpio always being one of my biggest blessings. He changed me for the better and showed me what real love was. To think... All of this came to me because I'd been *Scorned By The Love Of A Thug.*

(The End...)